"No One Ever Kissed Me Like That."

He didn't want to hear that. Even a lamb should have more sense than to admit her vulnerability to a wolf. Guilt pummeled through him. He should never have touched her. "Nothing happened," he said sharply.

"Maybe not for you." Her smile was soft, teasing.

Zach was briefly inclined to tear his hair out by the roots. "Kirstin," he said patiently, "we're alone in this house. When a guy that you don't know from Adam comes on to you, in a place where you could shout from here to Atlanta and never be heard, you're supposed to knock his block off."

"Well, I'll remember that next time," she murmured.

Those Connor brothers don't stand a chance of staying single—once they cross the threshold and become JOCK'S BOYS.

Dear Reader,

Every month we try to bring you something exciting in Silhouette Desire, and this month is no exception.

First, there's the *Man of the Month* by Jennifer Greene, which *also* is the start of a charming new miniseries by this award-winning writer. The book is *Bewitched* and the series is called JOCK'S BOYS after the delightful, meddlesome ghost of an old sea pirate.

Next, Jackie Merritt's sinfully sexy series about the Saxon Brothers continues with *Mystery Lady*. Here, brother Rush Saxon meets his match in alluring ice princess Valentine LeClaire.

Lass Small hasn't run out of Brown siblings yet! In *I'm Gonna Get You*, Tom Brown learns that you can't always get who you want when you want her....

Suzanne Simms has always been asked by her friends, "Why don't you write some funny books?" So, Suzanne decided to try and *The Brainy Beauty*—the first book in her HAZARDS, INC. series—is the fun-filled result.

And so you don't think that miniseries books are the only thing we do, look for *Rafferty's Angel* by up-and-coming writer Caroline Cross. And don't miss Donna Carlisle's *Stealing Savannah*, about a suave ex-jewel thief and the woman who's out to get him.

Sincerely,

Lucia Macro
Senior Editor

Please address questions and book requests to:
Reader Service
U.S.: P.O. Box 1325, Buffalo, NY 14269
Canadian: P.O. Box 1050, Niagara Falls, Ont. L2E 7G7

JENNIFER
GREENE
BEWITCHED

SILHOUETTE *Desire*

Published by Silhouette Books

America's Publisher of Contemporary Romance

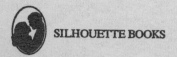

SILHOUETTE BOOKS

ISBN 0-373-05847-0

BEWITCHED

Printed in U.S.A.

Books by Jennifer Greene

Silhouette Desire

Body and Soul #263
Foolish Pleasure #293
Madam's Room #326
Dear Reader #350
Minx #366
Lady Be Good #385
Love Potion #421
The Castle Keep #439
Lady of the Island #463
Night of the Hunter #481
Dancing in the Dark #498
Heat Wave #553
Slow Dance #600
Night Light #619
Falconer #671
Just Like Old Times #728
It Had To Be You #756
Quicksand #786
*Dewitched #847

Silhouette Intimate Moments

Secrets #221
Devil's Night #305
Broken Blossom #345
Pink Topaz #418

Silhouette Books

Birds, Bees and Babies 1990
"Riley's Baby"

*Jock's Boys

JENNIFER GREENE

lives near Lake Michigan with her husband and two children. Before writing full-time, she worked as a personnel manager, teacher and college counselor. Michigan State University honored her as an "outstanding woman graduate" for her work with women on campus.

Ms. Greene has written over thirty-five category romances for which she has won many awards, including the Rita for "Best Short Contemporary" book from Romance Writers of America and "Best Series Author" from *Romantic Times*.

Prologue

Jock heard a door slam below, and hastened to look out of the third-story window. Finally! The first of the Connor boys had arrived.

He took a studying look at the lad. Zach was this one's name. He was standing next to some kind of sleek black contraption— shiny enough, but a cracker box in size. It was impossible to comprehend how a man's long legs would fit inside. And the lad was definitely long, uncommonly tall with a braw set of broad shoulders...but so thin. Jock guessed his age at thirty, no more. Wild black curly hair and a matching full beard. Jock knew precisely how long it took to grow a good healthy beard—he had one himself—but the lad's was unkempt, and his face had a winter pallor.

The lad looked up—seeing nothing in the window, of course—but Jock could see him. Even from the distance of three stories, he could see the lad's eyes.

Burning blue they were. Burning blue with the fire of exhaustion. Burning blue like there was a hole in his soul.

Well. Jock straightened with a frown, his hand automatically folding on the jewel-crusted handle of his sword. The lad was in rough shape, no doubt about that. If it were only the year of our Lord 1723, he'd take the lad to sea and stuff the boy with vittles and rum. It'd be easy enough to build him up in the stout salt air.

Regretfully that was not an option, but Jock was undaunted. He'd find a way to strengthen the boy. It couldn't be that hard. Fresh air and exercise would surely cure the pallor. The bone structure was true; the face had clean strong lines beneath the bearlike beard, and there wasn't a woman born who could ignore those eyes. Whether he was any kind of lover, Jock couldn't guess, but that wasn't a problem.

He would help instruct the lad on technique, when it was time.

Jock turned away from the window, thinking hard. His first problem, of course, was finding a woman. Not a virgin. It was almost impossible to find a virgin at this point in the twentieth century. More relevant, a virgin in *any* century wasn't half the fun of a lass who knew what she was doing between the sheets. No, this Zach needed a woman with some experience. A woman with a little sass and spirit in her character. Preferably buxom with some solid meat on her bones.

Jock didn't like skinny women, and since he fully intended to watch the action—most of the action—he might as well find a woman who fit his personal liking.

He rubbed his hands together, already feeling the excitement of anticipation.

Damned if he didn't feel alive again.

The lad looked like someone had torn the soul right out of him, but Jock wasn't one to dwell on inconsequentials. He had a role to fulfill in the lad's life, and no earthly problems were likely to stop him. He'd fix the lad up just fine.

He'd fix them all.

He watched with satisfaction as the lad hefted his gear and hiked the snow-strewn grass for the house. A few more steps. That's all it would take.

Once Zach crossed the threshold, he was one of Jock's boys.

One
***

When Zachary Connor climbed out of the sleek black Lotus, the bitter salt air stung his eyes. Maine weather in November clearly had nothing in common with L.A. The wind whipping off the Atlantic was colder than chipped ice...and howling like a mournful ghost.

Shivering hard, he glanced around. The house was perched on an ice-swept knoll. Past the house, the yard sledded down a rolling slope to the rocky shore. A tall white lighthouse loomed in the distance, clearly defunct and abandoned. Waves sputtered and spit on the wet rocks. He saw rooftops along the jagged edge of coast—with only a few miles to Bar Harbor, he was obviously stuck with neighbors—but thankfully none too close.

The tension in his shoulders eased. Everything about the view relieved his mind. All he wanted from life right now was to be left alone. Totally, completely alone.

The keyboard and case for his tenor sax were wedged in the front seat of the car, his knapsack jammed in back. He crossed to the passenger side to drag out his gear, but his attention strayed back to the house.

The old monster had to be two hundred years old. She'd been a beauty once. Still was. Although she had an empty, deserted air, she hadn't been neglected. The foundation was white frame with dark green shutters, both freshly painted, and she sprawled three stories tall with a widow's walk wrapped around the top level. The widows's walk made him suspect that a whaler or ship captain had built her years ago. A porch jutted out from the second floor with a view of the pounding ocean. An octagonal-shaped turret faced east with long, skinny windows. A weathered hex sign banged in the wind. No lights. The windows stared back at him with dark eyes.

Zach frowned. For an instant he thought he glimpsed movement from one of the tall upstairs windows, but that was absurd. His pulse rate climbed back down. No one was here or anywhere around. Although nothing was falling down, the whole place had an abandoned atmosphere, as if no one had lived here in years.

The house, like the view, suited him perfectly.

After fishing the house key from his jeans back pocket, he grabbed his gear and trudged toward the front door. The old brass key twisted in the lock. Like the campy sound effects of a Frankenstein movie, the huge oak door creaked open.

Dust motes and silence greeted him. Light poured into a castle-size hall. A two-landing open staircase—mahogany, he guessed—led upstairs. Doors opened on both sides below.

The first room off the right was an old-fashioned parlor—wing chairs, a horsehair couch, a frayed Persian rug, a lamp with a shade dripping fringe. The room was cozy warm. Someone had turned on the heat and piled a neat stack of logs by the huge, rough stone fireplace. Zach told himself that neither the warmth nor the furnishings should have surprised him. Both his brothers had told him that the place had a caretaker. Those kinds of details had been clearly spelled out in their grandfather's will. He hadn't paid any attention.

He couldn't imagine his grandfather living here. His two brothers had been equally mystified. None of them had expected this white elephant of an inheritance when Gramps died. No one in the family had ties in Maine. Seth and Michael speculated that their grandfather must have kept a woman here. It would have been like the rascally, unprincipled old codger. The mystery had fascinated his brothers. Not him.

Zach didn't care. For now, he was just grateful to have a place where no one could conceivably know or bother him.

Without taking off his leather jacket, he stowed his instruments and knapsack, and aimed for the hearth in the first parlor room. Crouching down, he stacked the logs and kindling, then thumbed open a matchbook. The fire took, first a lick of flame, then the whoosh when it really caught. Hungry yellow tongues lapped the dry wood. The air filled with the scent of smoky cedar and pine.

He hunched there, letting the fire mesmerize him, knowing there were things he should do. Exploring the house was an obvious priority. Because one room had furniture didn't mean there were automatically beds in the house. Food was a more serious problem. He'd found no place open to stop—hardly surprising on Thanksgiving morning—but somehow he had to find a way to lay in some supplies.

He hadn't eaten since last night, hadn't slept a full night since he could remember. He should be hungry, yet wasn't. He should care about finding a bed, yet didn't. None of it mattered. Nothing had mattered in months.

A telephone jangled from some distant room. Zach winced at the jarring noise, but didn't budge. He should have guessed that his brothers would make sure a phone was hooked up. It rang again. And again. Then finally, blessedly, quit.

They couldn't know that he'd arrived yet. He'd call them, but not until he could fake a healthy, hearty tone of voice. His brothers weren't easy to fool. At the funeral, Michael had been shocked at his appearance. Seth, who never wasted time on tact, had told him in explicit four-letter words to quit burning the candle at both ends. Both brothers had conned him into coming here and checking out this unexpected inheritance from Gramps, manufacturing the excuse that neither of them had the time. They were worried about him, Zach knew, and both believed he'd been working too hard. The two had conspired, as thick as thieves, both convinced that a restful, quiet month on the ocean would do him good.

Zach hadn't argued. He hadn't told them yet that he'd quit the band, that overwork was the exact opposite of his problem. He hadn't worked, couldn't work. The music wouldn't come. If his brothers understood how deeply he'd sunk into depression, they'd have been at his side faster than ants at a picnic, and no way they'd have let him be alone here. Zach didn't want them worried about him. It wasn't as if they could help. No one could help him.

His eyes burned from staring so long at the fire, yet he was afraid to close them.

Every time he closed his eyes, he saw a child's face. A baby. A baby's innocent, soft white face with his blue eyes. In the dead of night, every night, he heard her cry. The baby was alive, but he didn't know where. He didn't know if she was hungry, if she was healthy or hurt, if she needed something, if anyone loved her.

And he'd never know.

Guilt ripped through him, as familiar and sharp as the edge on a razor blade. God, if a man could die from guilt, he already would have. He could find no peace. His heart was a black abyss, a swallowing big hole with jagged edges. He didn't fight the pain, recognizing with harsh, bitter clarity that he deserved it. There was no healing this kind of raw wound. There wasn't supposed to be. The emptiness was corrosive, consuming. The only dependable staple in his life had been music—hell, music was the only part of his soul that had ever been worth anything—and now, it was gone. He couldn't work, couldn't think, couldn't rest.

His vision blurred. Maybe he was only thirty, but he felt like a worn-out one hundred and ten. He'd never fathomed that a man could be this tired. Gut-tired. Give-up tired. Not-care-anymore-about-anything tired. The hot orange flames danced in front of his eyes. He imagined dying....

Someone, somewhere, started pounding on a door.

Zach blinked, then scowled in exasperation, but he didn't move. Seth was in Atlanta, Michael in Detroit; no one knew him in Maine. It could only be a stranger at the door. They'd leave. Just as an unanswered phone eventually quit ringing, whoever was out there would give up on him, too.

The distant pounding stopped. Zach had just breathed a sigh of relief when minutes later, knuckles rapped again—incessantly, obtrusively—this time on the front door. Gritting his teeth, he ignored that, too.

A key scraped in the lock. A gust of cold air, wafting from the front hall, made the fire crackle and hiss. "Yoo-hoo! Mr. Connor? Are you there?"

The feminine voice sounded appallingly cheerful. Zach rubbed a hand over his eyes. He didn't respond—there was still a chance his unwanted visitor wouldn't find him and give up. He should have known better. Fate was in no mood to be kind.

Not one, but two females appeared in the doorway.

The first was a three-foot squirt with a curly mop of black hair, a floppy orange cap, blue eyes and a pug nose burned red by the wind. A child. A little girl. Every muscle in his body clenched tight. He hadn't been able to look at a kid in months—any kid, but especially kids with black hair and blue eyes like his own—without feeling that scissor-sharp jab of pain in his gut. Did he need this?

"Mr. Connor?"

His gaze tore free from the child and focused on the woman. Since she had obviously spotted him, answering wasn't a choice. It was a little late to make his six-foot-two frame conveniently disappear. "Yeah. I'm Connor."

The woman promptly tripped over her own feet. Graceful, she was not, but it didn't stop her from barreling right in with a wreath of a welcoming smile. She had a bruise on her cheek, as bright as a hooker's eyeshadow, startling enough to make the thought zoom through Zach's mind that someone had hit her. He changed his mind when he saw her shin connect with a chair leg. She either needed glasses or she was a born klutz.

Zach wasn't prone to exaggeration. She wasn't his worst nightmare. It was just that for a man who desperately craved peace, quiet and solitude, she was a wincing-bright slam of life. No huge stature—he doubted she'd reach five and a half feet in a stretch—but no one was going to miss her in a crowd. Her ski jacket was a shocking pink, loud enough to wake the dead, and the navy-and-pink stocking cap barely contained a short, exuberant froth of rusty brown curls. The jacket was flapping open, revealing a skinny figure in a yellow ribbed sweater and jeans. Truthfully he'd always been attracted to skinny women—but not now. At the moment his libido was as dead as his heart, and the last thing on earth he wanted was female company. Especially overbright, overcheerful, *noisy* female company. She jarred his nerves like the sharps of an untuned piano. Worse, she took one quick look at him and started talking.

Started.

And wouldn't quit.

"Heavens! You must have just gotten here, haven't even had the chance to take off your coat. I'm sorry. I'm Kirstin Grams, and this is my daughter Amelia Anne—Mellie. I've been caretaking the place for the last year... frankly I was beginning to wonder if anyone was ever going to enjoy this wonderful old place! Isn't it a terrific house? I'm so glad you're here. Seth Connor called me—I assume he's your brother? And when he said you were due here today, I started to worry that you wouldn't find any place to buy food on the holiday. We've got a Thanksgiving feast set up at my house. You're more than welcome if you'd like to come. And I need to ask what you want me to do. I mean... none of the house is really opened up. Until I met you face-to-face, I had no idea what you wanted done—"

"Stop." Apparently that soft, wide mouth came with an ever-ready battery. Once she wound up, she could enthusiastically run on without ever needing a breath. Zach needed to catch his. His head was pounding like a freight train.

Her infernal good cheer was as welcome as a case of food poisoning. Rudeness was obviously the quickest route to getting rid of her, but the kid was staring at him with those round blue eyes, and he couldn't bring himself to be outright mean in front of the kid. Especially a kid with such a witless mother.

Kirstin Grams, did she say her name was? On one hand, Zach told himself to be grateful that the indubitable Ms. Grams didn't appear to recognize him. Not that rhythm and blues was everyone's raison d'être, but his band had scored handfuls of hits over the years. As a result, his face had been plastered in more tabloids than he cared to count. Notoriety was a lot easier to come by than anonymity.

Still, if she *didn't* recognize him, she was on the fruitcake side of nuts to ask him to dinner. Zach knew what he looked like. The long hair and gold stud in his ear was *de rigueur* in the music world—no different than the Wall Street uniform was pinstripes—but he'd paid no attention to his appearance in months. The wild black hair and unruly beard, the earring and old cracked leather jacket—he had to look like a vagrant on drugs or an escaped con on the lam. And she was blithely asking him to dinner? Dinner with her little kid, yet?

"Thanks for the offer, but I don't need dinner. Or anything else," he said flatly. If the dead tone didn't get his message across, the dark scowl should have.

She didn't budge. The wide cheerful smile didn't even waver. "You're sure? We really have more than enough, and if you've been driving all day you must be tired. I'll tell you what! When the turkey's done, I'll just bring over a plate. We're just a few miles down the road, so it really isn't any bother—"

God. She was winding up again. With deliberate slowness, Zach lurched to his feet. He'd lost weight these past months. Even so, standing straight, he had an intimidating six inches and a good sixty pounds on her. She couldn't fail to notice. Yet when he purposefully loomed toward her, she only winsomely cocked her head.

"I make a mean apple pie. You'll love it. And do you like your stuffing with raisins or not? My dad loves raisins, but Mellie can't stand them, so I always make both kinds—"

Enough was enough. He cut in. "Thank you. I don't want dinner. I don't want anything. I appreciate your coming by."

The dismissal was as obvious as a pitcher's hardball. It rolled right past her. "—and when I bring dinner, I really need to ask about what you want done. No one was living here before. Harvey Bennett is the lawyer who hired me—I never met him, except over the phone—but all he wanted me to do was watch over the place. Have someone regularly walk through, make sure the lawn was mowed and the snow was plowed, move a few things around so it would look like someone was here. You know how an empty house has a tendency to walk away? I caretake several of the vacation homes around Bar Harbor the same way, especially in the wintertime—"

There was no point in trying to interrupt her. He figured the chances were better for peace in the Middle East than of his getting a word in. He made a motion, like shooing a cat. The little one picked up on it and tugged on her mother's hand. Kirstin started backing out of the room with the child in tow—although none too quickly. Zach felt like an exasperated wolf stuck with the ironic job of herding two hapless lambs to safety. He didn't want to show his teeth, but by God, his head was splitting wide open with the mother of all headaches. What was it going to take to make her disappear?

"—and maybe you'll want me to quit that, now that you're here, but you've probably seen the dustcovers all over the house. I'm afraid it's been years since the whole place had a serious sorting and cleaning. If you want the help, the best I could do is Tuesday and Friday afternoons. Of course, maybe you want to do the whole thing yourself—"

Zach had never met such an exhaustingly cheerful or talkative woman, and if fate was kind, he never would again. Still, halfway to the front door, her last comment dented his exasperation. He didn't particularly care if the whole house rotted, but this was his brothers' inheritance as well as his. Technically he was here to check out the place and put it in order, so the three of them could decide what to do with it. At the moment Zach didn't have the energy to eat, much less physically handle this monster of a white elephant alone.

"Tuesdays and Fridays, you said?" The question sneaked out before he could bite his tongue. The knives shooting through his skull made it hard to think. There was no way Zach wanted anyone around, much less a woman who'd managed to singlemind-edly drive him batty in ten short minutes. But even a quick glance at the yawning huge house was depressing. He was exhausted to the bone, knew damn well he needed help, and at least she was the devil he knew. The idea of having to advertise and interview a passel of strangers for the work was untenable. And how hard could it be to stay out of her sight for those two afternoons a week? "I don't know. I'll have to think about it."

"Fine. Whatever you want is okay with me. Just let me know, and we'd better get back to Grandpa, shouldn't we, Mellie.... I'm so glad to meet you, Mr. Connor." She shot out her hand, chuckled, removed a fuzzy pink mitten and shot out her hand again.

He took it. Her palm was warm, damp, and as soft as a baby's behind. Her eyes zipped to his. For an instant he was close enough to see the dance of freckles on her nose, the arch of pale brows, the fragile bones set in a delicate oval face.

It was the first time she'd quit moving and talking long enough for him to realize she was cute. Not gorgeous, not glamorous, but definitely cute in a wholesome, natural kind of way. Zach couldn't remember the last time he'd met a woman who didn't use face paint and perfume. Her skin was a flawless ivory and her eyes were a strikingly clear, dark blue.

Unfortunately there was something in those deep, dark eyes...something warm, something as basic and simple as kindness. A frisson of uneasiness chased up Zach's spine. It was much, much easier, holding on to his first impression that she was a witless babbler, than worrying that she'd taken one look at him and gone the long mile to be nice.

He didn't want to be anywhere near a *nice* woman, and he sure as hell didn't want kindness. Not from her. Not from anyone. He pumped her hand, once, then dropped it faster than a hot coal and yanked open the front door. Frigid air poured in, along with that howling noisy wind.

She smiled. "I'll be back with dinner," she promised him.

"No."

He pealed out a second "No," but still couldn't be positive that she heard him. The two had already bounded off his porch and were scrambling, heads down, for a rust heap of an ancient orange pickup with flower decals.

Zach kicked the door closed and then leaned flat against it with his eyes closed. The whole encounter hadn't lasted fifteen minutes. He felt more whipped than a battered dog. If she'd stayed any longer, he was afraid he'd have torn her head off. Hurt her feelings. And then felt even more like a guilty bastard than he did now, but damnation, all he wanted was to be left alone. Isolation. Silence. Solitude. Was that too much to ask from life?

"By the saints, you sure made a frigging mess of that."

Zach's eyes popped open. He heard the voice—a man's low cracked baritone—but it seemed to come from nowhere.

"I should probably introduce myself. The name's Jock. Never had a last name, never missed one, and 'twouldn't be relevant to ye anyhow. But to get back to the lass..."

Zach scalped a hand through his hair. As humorous, ridiculous and idiotic as it sounded...that baritone actually sounded real.

"She was a bit scrawny, I'll give you that, not what I had in mind for you a'tall. But ye had to notice she had a sweet round fanny under those breeches. Skin as soft as a cloud. Eyes that made a man want to peel down the sheets. She was hot for you, lad. I know about these things. She took one look at ye and was thinking about a cuddle. Are ye blind? Need spectacles? Ye were mean, ye were, near kicked her out the door. Lar, ye're going to make my job near impossible if we don't shape up your attitude. I'm disgusted with ye, and that's the God's truth.''

Zach spun around. There was no one. Anywhere. No shadow, no footstep, no sign of any presence but that voice.

At the far end of the hall, there was a long plate-glass mirror, ornately framed and dusty with age. For an instant he thought he saw an image in it. A man. Long black glossy hair, wearing pirate's gear and long boots, a roll of fat around his belt and a sword hanging near his thigh. The image was there. Wavy, dusty, but real. And then gone.

Zach let out an exasperated sigh. He was depressed. That wasn't news. The depth of his depression wasn't a new headline, either, and chronic lack of sleep could make any man imagine things. Still, he just wasn't the type to indulge in this kind of weirdness. He'd always been a hard-bitten realist, hardly a believer in spirits or psychic nonsense—and none too patient or tolerant with those who did.

At least until now, he hadn't sunk so low as to dream up voices or imagine ghosts.

He should probably be seriously worried about his sanity. Instead, his mouth twitched with dark, dry humor. A ghost was likely the only companion who could put up with him right now. God knew, he wasn't fit company for man or beast...and definitely not for a woman.

Unbidden and unwanted, a mental image of Kirstin drifted back through his mind. She was a talking plague, a chatterbox, and her incessant, bubbly friendliness had nearly exhausted him. But he'd been curiously taken with her. Or he might have been. If meeting her hadn't inexorably reminded him that he didn't belong anywhere near a wholesome, pink-cheeked woman with the innocence of kindness in her eyes. Zach had known a lot of women. None of them had been wholesome. None, remotely innocent. And neither was he.

The sins on his conscience suddenly weighed heavier than tombstones. Head down, he wandered back to his fire.

He promptly forgot about Ms. Grams. Nothing could have been easier, since there wasn't a chance on this earth that he'd touch a woman like Kirstin with a ten-foot pole.

She couldn't possibly be a problem for him.

Two

"Best Thanksgiving dinner I've ever had, Kirstin. You should have been a chef. You're an even better cook than your mother was." Paul Stone looked straight into his daughter's eyes. Under the table, he opened a napkin where Mellie promptly dumped her peas. "Did I tell you John and Bette Simskon just flew to Europe?"

"The Simskons? I thought they were divorced."

"They are. Never should have married in the first place. They've gotten on like a houseafire ever since the divorce was final. Bette claimed he was taking her to the Orient after this. Oh, look." Paul beamed at Mellie. "She's finished all her vegetables. Aren't you a good girl! I guess she rates a big piece of apple pie, don't you, punkin?"

Kirstin cupped her chin in a palm. "I suppose you think just because it's Thanksgiving, that I'm going to let you two get away with murder?"

"Does that mean Mom's onto us?" Mellie whispered to her grandfather.

"It's pretty hard to trick your mother. I've told you before, she's got eyes in the back of her head."

"No, she doesn't, Grandpa. I looked ages ago. I looked and looked. All she's got is hair and head back there. You made that up."

"Me? Make up stories?" Paul leaned back from the table, leaving room for Mellie to climb onto his lap, and launched into another tall tale while Kirstin carted dishes to the sink. He waited, but no dessert appeared. "You're not going to deprive us of pie just because of one small fib, are you?"

Kirstin chuckled. "You'll get it in a minute, not to worry. Before I put everything away, I just wanted to fix a plate to take to Mr. Connor. I don't think he had an ounce of food in that house."

"You're like your mother in that, too. Can't remember a holiday she wasn't giving away good food to strangers. It's a genetic flaw passed down on the women's side, Mellie, you'll have to watch for it. And we sat down to dinner so fast that neither one of you mentioned what you thought of this new neighbor of ours."

Kirstin sliced the pie, not needing to answer because her daughter did.

"He had a cool car," Mellie volunteered. "Black and shiny. And he had a beard. It was black, too. I liked him."

"Did you now?"

Mellie nodded. "He looks like a big ol' growly bear. Even bigger than you, Grandpa."

"That big, hmm?" Paul's gaze shifted to his daughter when she served the pie. "Did you find out where he's from, what he does for a living?"

"There was hardly time to poke and pry. We were only there a few minutes." More than long enough, Kirstin thought, to form an indelibly strong impression of Zachary Connor. But she wasn't about to share that impression with her father.

They all rose from the table minutes later, but she couldn't leave the kitchen a disaster. Scruff and Muff tangled around her legs as she cleaned up—both cats knew she had turkey. She fed them scraps in between handling the leftovers and washing up, but her glance kept straying to the window.

It wasn't that late—just past six—but the sky was already jet-black. Snow danced in the air. Flutter flakes. By morning the yard would be dusted and the leafy pines would be laced with white. The sugar maples near the back door were already coated with hoar frost. It was a night to curl up by a sleepy-warm fire, toasting her toes and relaxing.

Instead, she planned to galivant off in the dark to chase down a man who had already made clear that he didn't want her food—or her company.

As she wiped the last counter, Kirstin told herself she was nuts. The epitaph rang annoyingly true. Still, she grabbed her jacket, plugged the mounded plate in the microwave to reheat and paused in the doorway.

"I'm just going to take the food over. I won't be long."

"You want some company? We could all go."

Kirstin shook her head. Mellie was installed next to him, holding a Mercer Mayer book and a floppy-eared moose, her favorite stuffed animal. They'd started a fire, turned on the TV with the volume low. Lamplight made buttery-soft shadows on the pine walls. "You two are all settled in. I'll be fine, Dad, really. And I'll be back in two shakes."

"You sure you want to go alone?"

"I'm sure." A total fabrication, she thought dryly. She wasn't sure at all. And the instant she stepped outside, the frigid air burned her cheeks. When the wind dropped earlier, the temperature had plummeted. It wasn't just cold, but bitter-mean cold. Maine-November cold. The moonless night was blacker than a witch's heart.

Shivering wildly, she climbed into the truck, set the plate of food on the seat and promptly banged her elbow on the steering wheel. In the next life she was going to be as graceful as a dancer. In this life, divine intervention couldn't seem to save her from klutziness. Nursing her elbow, she fumbled to insert the ignition key. The old Ford was willing to start in winter. If she coaxed and begged it. Once the engine coughed to life, of course, the windows had to be scraped free of frost.

It was a lot of trouble to go through, for a man who'd been as friendly as a cornered skunk. Enough trouble to make a woman doubt her sanity, and her fingers were pinch-frozen by the time she climbed back into the truck and took off. Not surprisingly, there wasn't a soul on the roads. Everyone else, on Thanksgiving night, had the sense to be home with their fam-

ilies, curled up where it was warm and snug and safe.
Not her.

She caught her reflection in the rearview mirror.
Last week, she'd walked into the hairdresser for a cut
and come out with a short, frizz-fest of a new permanent. The stylist had talked her into it. Kirstin had
taken one look at the results and wondered what she'd
ever done to the woman. The bruise on her cheek was
finally fading—a result of an unexpected confronta-
tion with a closed door, nothing exciting—but apart
from the appallingly silly curls and the bruise, she
looked normal. Blue eyes, clean skin, the same familiar wide mouth and even, ordinary features. There was
nothing in her reflection to indicate a sudden,
alarming problem with insanity.

Kirstin had the gloomy premonition that Zach was
going to slam the door in her face, yet she kept driving. She never walked down dark alleys alone at night,
and at twenty-nine years old, she certainly knew better than to tangle with strange men—especially men
who made her feel restless and nervous and edgy. Yet
that didn't make her turn around, either.

It wasn't often that Kirstin let impulse rule her ac-
tions, but she had her moments. Alan was one of
them. Her husband had been quiet and reserved, av-
erage in looks and with such a tepid personality that
none of the women in the office had looked at him
twice. When he asked her out, she'd almost turned
him down, positive they would never find anything to
talk about. She'd been so wrong. Alan had been an
angel of a lover in bed, a sensitive and perceptive man
who had easily come out of his shell in a loving relationship.

Kirstin had no reason to think that Zachary Connor was anything like her husband. But a combination of marriage, life and love had taught her to trust her natural feminine instincts. Sometimes a woman simply had to follow the impulses of her heart, and Zach had definitely aroused some powerful feminine impulses.

When she walked into the house that afternoon, she'd fully expected to see a man who'd been physically ill from overwork. Both his brothers, Seth and Michael, had telephoned her that morning. They'd called before, asking specifics about the house, but this was a more personal call. Neither had heard from Zach. They'd wanted to know if she'd seen him, if he'd arrived safely, because it was such a long drive from the coast and he'd been ill. Kirstin hadn't thought any more about it until she'd laid eyes on Zach.

Maybe he'd been physically ill from overwork—his brothers should certainly know. But she didn't believe it.

It had been six years now since she lost her mother. And then Alan, just two years back. Most people saw her as an incorrigible optimist—she usually had a smile for the world—but her life had never been a carnival ride. Kirstin knew what loss was. She knew how crippling grief could be. She knew what it was to wake up in the morning, feeling like a dagger was stuck in her heart, afraid to move, afraid to breathe, afraid to think for being ambushed by memories.

That kind of pain had been in Zach's eyes. Maybe not grief, but some kind of unbearable emotional blow. Initially his looks had intimidated her. The

Harley-type leather jacket and earring and unruly
black hair—he looked like he was fresh from a mo-
torcycle gang, dangerous and reckless and hardly her
type. Within minutes, though, she hadn't cared what
"type" he was. She couldn't stop looking at those
fierce, wild, empty blue eyes.

It wasn't as if she felt responsible for him. She
didn't. She wasn't. And it wasn't as if she knew him—
there was no specific *reason* for her to worry that the
man was going to sit in that house and starve. But he
had no family in Maine, no one to turn to if he were
in trouble, and Kirstin had always had certain weak-
nesses. She'd never been able to ignore a crying baby.
She'd always been a sucker for even the mangiest stray.
And she was simply incapable of deserting another
human being who was in pain.

Seconds later she pulled into his driveway, parking
where she had that afternoon. She switched off the
key, then the lights, grabbed the platter of food and
climbed out.

Abruptly her heart started pounding. Her palms
dampened, slidey-slick with nerves. Out of nowhere,
she suddenly felt as shaky as if she were standing on
the edge of a jagged cliff with no rail in sight.

Stuff and nonsense. Firmly she squared her shoulders. There was nothing to be afraid of. Naturally
Zach had stirred a few feminine nerves—he was an
intimidatingly potent male package—but she wasn't
nervous around men, never had been. She'd worked
in the business world, was the responsible single mom
of a seven-year-old. She could handle herself. The
worst that could happen was that he'd turn down the
food and be rude. Big deal.

She propped on a smile and resolutely hiked for the door. A little late, she noticed that the wonderful old house was as pitch-dark as a cave.

God. What now? Whoever was pounding on the door was as persistent as a mosquito. Wielding an ungainly long flashlight, Zach stalked down the hall and yanked open the front door. Even in the sooty shadows, he immediately recognized the neon pink jacket.

Her again. Ms. Innocence with the appallingly sweet smile. A pithy four-letter word sprang to mind, but Zach bit it back with an impatient sigh. His mood rivaled an ornery porcupine's, but that was hardly her fault. Hell, he could have guessed she'd be back. He'd left her hanging about the job. From the look of her rust-bitten truck, she needed the work, and after spending the past four hours in the blasted house, Zach had come to the tediously annoying conclusion that he needed her. As long as she wasn't counting on a friendly employer—and he'd make *damn* sure he kept a careful distance—she could have the answer she wanted in two seconds flat.

"You didn't have to drive back. I would have called you," he clipped out. "Yeah, you can come Tuesday and Friday afternoons. More if you've got the time. And I don't care what you charge."

"Fifty bucks an hour."

"Fine."

Her brows arched in surprise, followed by the tip of a mischievous grin. "That was a joke, Mr. Connor. I promise my terms are a lot fairer than that. And thanks, I'm glad to hear about the job, but the real reason I came was to bring you some dinner...is there some reason why it's so dark in here?"

"I like it dark." Heaven knew why he bothered answering. She hadn't paid any attention to his repressive leave-me-alone scowls before, and she didn't now.

"Something *must* be wrong, or you wouldn't be carrying that flashlight." Quick as a blink, she was in and thrusting a heavy platter into his hands. Unprepared, he'd have dropped it if she hadn't absconded with his flashlight at the same time. "You blew a fuse, didn't you? And a big one. I can help you with that. I'm used to the old-fashioned electrical systems in these old houses...."

She would doubtless have gone on, if the front door hadn't suddenly closed as if pushed by an unseen hand. Her gaze leaped from the door to him.

"A gust of wind," Zach said flatly. Her lips parted to say something else when there was another sound— the unmistakable click of a key turning in a lock. Both of them were standing three feet away from the door, and that time, she jumped.

"Damn," Zach muttered.

"Did that door lock itself or did I imagine it?" She gave an uneasy laugh, and then quickly shook her head. "Sorry. Sometimes I tend to get spooked in the dark. The amount of time I've spent in old houses, you'd think I'd know about creaks and bumps in the night. And no matter. I'm off to fix your fuse. Don't argue, okay?—I do this kind of thing all the time—it's no sweat for me—and there isn't anything on that plate that will stay warm long. You just eat. I'll be out of here in a jiffy."

That was most reassuring news. She strode blithely down the hall with his only source of light, which didn't bother Zach. But seconds later, he heard a wooden chair rattle and crash, followed by her low-pitched, "Ouch."

He pinched the bridge of his nose. He had a sudden, brief, terrifying vision of Ms. Kirstin-Klutzy-Grams breaking an ankle and being stranded in his house for hours. He moved. Fast.

She knew where the fuse box was. So did he. Hidden in the godforsaken back of a long pantry off the kitchen. There was no basement in the house; it had nearly taken him a half hour to find the unexpected little room in the dark. Then another twenty minutes glaring at the antiquated electrical system with the wavering flashlight. There had to be two hundred fuses. Eventually he'd have figured out which one was the problem. Maybe. By next Tuesday.

When he caught up with her, she'd already peeled off her jacket and was rummaging noisily in her purse with the flashlight flickering every which way. Her hand emerged with a yellow-and-orange electrical tester, making him wonder what else was in that suitcase-size purse.

"You don't have to do this," he said testily.

"Of course I don't. And I know you could have handled it yourself." Her husky alto was as calming as a tranquilizer. That tone implied a wealth of experience at soothing male egos before, an idea that rasped on his nerves. "How's that turkey? It was hot when I left, and the drive only took a few minutes, but it was really freezing in the truck."

She'd piled the food in some kind of insulated plate. It was still warm in his hands. He wasn't hungry, but a peak of the plastic cover had worked free when she handed it to him. He could smell turkey. And blueberry muffins. And honey-glazed carrots with a spice that his nose recognized—cinnamon?

When the fuse blew, he'd been heating water for coffee on the stove. The only nonclothes items in his knapsack were coffee—because he was fussy about brands—and a tall bottle of Chivas. He'd planned to go to bed with that scotch. Now he wished he'd already opened the bottle.

She provided a steady stream of small talk—had his brothers reached him? Could he believe how cold it was outside tonight?—as she moved the electrical tester from fuse to fuse. Her slim figure was outlined every time she lifted her arms. The ribbed yellow sweater didn't hide much. She could be a Hepburn sister, nothing at all upstairs, but her jeans cupped a sassy little fanny and snugly outlined her long skinny legs.

He forced his gaze above her neck. She'd forgotten her hat tonight. He'd caught a glimpse of her red-brown hair that afternoon, but now he could see the cap of springy, wild curls. The color was less red than a rich, dark paprika, tucked around the shell of her ears and curling around her throat, and so thick that a man's hands could get lost in it.

"You must have explored the house by now...isn't it something? It always killed me that no one lived here for so long. The alcoves and window seats and thick stucco ceilings and wainscoting...everything has so much character, so much history. I'm pretty sure she was built around the time of whaling ships..."

Abruptly the lights flickered on, followed by the rumbling thud of the furnace. She stopped talking long enough to smile at him—an exultant grin of success, as potent as a dose of pure liquid sunshine—and he saw the bruise on her cheek again. It was small, never some huge or dangerous injury, but the motley color was such a contrast to her clear, white skin. He had the strangest protective urge to touch that bruise. Her mouth had no lip color, no gloss. Her lips were naked, as smooth as the petals on a rose. He wanted to touch that mouth, too. Just to know if the texture was really softer than butter. Just to find out if she could conceivably taste as sweet and vulnerable as she looked.

She tugged on his senses. Zach told himself there was an obvious reason for that. He didn't know anyone like her. The women he met through the music world had already dipped in sin and mistakes; they'd toughened up young and knew how to protect themselves. Not her, he thought. Her face was a moving X ray of emotion, and she didn't have the self-protective instincts of a goose. Her cheeks flushed with telling color when she looked at him. And when she suddenly tilted her chin, he saw big blue eyes and a land mine of feminine awareness and nerves. "Mr. Connor, there's something I should have discussed with you..."

"Make it Zach. I've been Mister-Connored about as much as I can stand."

"Zach, then..." She switched off the flashlight and took a breath. "If I work in the afternoons, some-

times I have to bring Mellie. She gets out of school at
two. My dad's been technically retired for a couple of
years—he had a small business, repairing fishing boats
in the harbor—but he still keeps his hand in, so I can't
always count on him to be there. If it's a problem for
you if I bring Mellie—''

"If you need to bring your daughter, bring your
daughter. It makes no difference to me." The men-
tion of her child was as effective as a splash of ice water. Abruptly he realized how long he'd been staring,
and that, impossibly, his body was aroused at no more
than the look of her. He could have sworn his hormones were dead. If not, they needed some fast,
ruthless zapping.

Her feelings for children were obvious. Every time
she mentioned Mellie, her face glowed with love and
warmth. She might be soft, but Zach had no doubt
she'd bite a bullet for her kid. He could too easily
imagine what she'd think of a man who would carelessly risk the future of a child.

He shifted restlessly when she eased past him out of
the pantry. She never touched him, but there was that
look in her eyes again. *It's just a little rush of chemistry, honey. Trust me, you'll get over it. I'm the last
man you'd want to tangle with, and I don't care how
cute you look in that skinny yellow sweater.*

He groped for something to say. "Thanks. For fix-
ing the fuse. I guess you have to be a jack-of-all-trades
if you caretake many houses." He should have known.
Give her any opening, and she leaped right in.

"My dad didn't believe in raising any helpless females. Actually, though, my field is computers. I was
a systems analyst in Albany for seven years. Then my

husband Alan died two years ago—an aneurysm, nothing anyone could have expected—and I think both Mellie and I were in shock for a while, so we came home to live with my dad. Most of the businesses around here relate to either fishing or tourism. There wasn't enough work in my field to even keep us in peanut butter. I didn't exactly plan to turn into a caretaker, but it's worked out. A lot of people have vacation homes on the coast, feel uneasy at leaving their places empty for the long winter months..." She chuckled suddenly. "You're just like Mellie. You like carrots but not peas."

"I wasn't..." He started to say he wasn't hungry, but then he glanced down. Except for a scoopful of peas, the white platter with the Wedgwood blue rim was empty.

"You were starving," she said gently. "I'm glad I brought it over. Tomorrow, all the stores'll be open. Head north on the coast road, turn left on Mill. There's a corner grocer. You can almost walk to it. Rolf, who runs the place, is really a sweetheart..."

She never quit talking. He didn't want to hear her life story, didn't want to wonder about the kind of man she'd been married to, didn't want all this help. She fluttered around the redbrick kitchen, closing the white cupboard doors and drawers, the way a woman automatically set a kitchen to rights without thinking. He'd yanked everything open when he was looking for the flashlight. She spotted the tall amber bottle of scotch on the counter, glanced at him quickly, nervously, then away.

"You need some *food*. And I assume by now you've picked out a bedroom upstairs. I'll bet the huge one with the porch, right?"

"I haven't been upstairs." And he didn't necessarily intend to. After calling both his brothers, he'd spent hours rattling around all the empty rooms on the first floor. Pacing. The place had endless rooms. Rooms for nothing. Small, most of them. A library without books, a south sun room without plants, a second parlor and dining room, and the octagonal-shaped turret room with all windows. He'd left his instruments in the turret room and spent a few minutes alone with his tenor sax. A useless waste of time. He'd made sound, not music. The music wouldn't come, which should have been no surprise. He'd given up, and then paced some more.

Not for love or money could he seem to buy any peace, but at least he'd been alone and the whole place had been quiet.

Nothing about Ms. Grams was quiet.

"You're kidding! You haven't been upstairs? There's a second staircase up, a servants stairs. It winds down from the third floor. And there's a linen closet up there, behind a strange looking little curved door. It's loaded. Heaven knows who left all the stuff, but the sheets and blankets are covered in plastic. Not that anything will be fresh, but it should do until you have the chance to wash everything up. Or I can do that when I come on Tuesday—"

"Kirstin." He used her given name because it seemed the only way to catch her attention. She tilted her chin. The fuzz of curls framed her oval face, the delicate even features, the vulnerability in her blue eyes every time she looked at him. "You can't always be this friendly to strangers. You *can't* be."

"No." It was the first time she'd said anything slowly. But the single, short word came slow and a little tremulously. "You just seemed so...alone. And I'm sorry, I know I'm talking too much. It's a habit when I'm nervous and first meet someone—"

"Kirstin." The use of her first name worked again; she stopped talking. He said quietly, "Thank you for dinner. Thank you for helping with the fuse. But you need to go home now."

"Yes, of course. In fact, I was just leaving. My jacket..." She glanced around wildly. "I must have left my jacket in the pantry." She surged forward and promptly connected with the edge of the old pine table. She wasn't looking where she was going. She was looking at him.

The expression in her face was a lottery giveaway. God knew what appealed to her in his unkempt, derelict appearance, but something seemed to. Zach had known too many women not to recognize when one was attracted. He wanted to wash a weary hand over his face. It wasn't as if he was afraid of her coming on to him. He'd bet his life savings that Kirstin wasn't the kind to come on to any man. Nothing about her was overtly seductive or sexually aggressive. In spite of her bubbly gregariousness, he suspected that her down-deep values were as old-fashioned as a homemade apple pie.

But he really didn't like the way she looked at him. She seemed to have formed the instinctive feminine opinion that he was a good guy. Nice. Trustworthy. Worth knowing. A potential pal. God. The wrong man could take her for a rough ride so fast it would make her head spin.

She retrieved her jacket, awkwardly dived into it and then stood there.

"You need to go home," he repeated gently.

"Heavens, yes." It galvanized her into movement again. She rushed for the doorway, then backtracked. "My plate. I'd better take the plate; you don't want to have to wash it. And I'll be here Tuesday. One o'clock."

But she came to another standstill at the front door, holding that empty plate, looking at him. She was working up to say something else, he guessed. Probably something helpful, something sweet.

He could have kissed her. The thought popped into his mind and lodged there like a sliver. She was standing that close, with her face tipped toward him. It would have solved something, he thought, if he yanked her into his arms and roughly, ruthlessly crushed that fragile, soft mouth. He knew women. He knew what to do. The wrong kind of kiss would guarantee she thought twice about being so helpful to strange men again. It would have plainly showed her that he wasn't the *nice* man she seemed to think he was. He could have scared her, and it struck Zach that scaring her was really a superb idea.

He lifted his hand. She never moved. It would have been easy, so easy to give in to that impulse. Easier than stealing candy from a baby. She sensed no danger at all.

Hell. He couldn't seem to make himself do it. Clamping his jaws together, he jerked away from her, fumbled with the locked latch and pulled the door open. "Good night," he snapped.

She straightened quickly and then lowered her eyes. "Good night, Zach."

The minute she was out the door, he shoved it closed and threw the dead bolt.

The house was instantly silent. Her constant, incessant chatter had made him forget how dead silent the cavernous old house really was. Not that he cared. She was gone, thank heavens. He could forget about her now.

He switched off the light in the hall, then the dining room. The bottle of scotch was waiting to be opened. If he chugged enough of it, eventually he'd sleep. If he didn't catch some sleep soon, he was going to lose his mind. Mentally he planned to collect the bottle, stoke the fire in the parlor and set up some kind of bedroll on the floor in there. Yet instead of moving, he found himself staring through the long beveled-glass window in the dark dining room.

Her truck was just pulling out, its headlights winking blindly in the night. She'd come out in the cold just for him. It bothered him, grated like a fingernail scraping on a chalkboard. *You just seemed so...alone*, she'd said. As if she knew anything about him.

She knew nothing.

Absolutely nothing.

"Did ye see the way she looked at ye?"

Zach's head swiveled around. That masculine low baritone of a voice again. A dusty lace curtain stirred near another window, but there was no one there. No shadow, no body, no nothing.

"She's been in the house a'fore, but I never thought of her for you. Somehow I thought ye'd go for a wilder, more experienced woman, but now I can see I was wrong. She appealed to ye, didn't she, lad? You were hard as a rock when you were looking at her. And it'd be nothing to get her in bed. She's the kind to think with her heart. Impulsive, that one. And a long time since she's been with a man, I'd be guessing. Easy prey for a good bedding..."

Zach spun on his heels. Nothing. No one. The voice, the hazy pirate image in the mirror, the front door suddenly locking when Kirstin arrived... he'd been damn sure it was all his imagination. Again, it struck his sense of humor that his mind had conjured up a ghost for company. The whole thing was funny. So funny he was tempted to laugh.

"...not much bosom, and there's a disappointment, but she'll strip better than ye'd believe, lad. Legs long enough to wrap tight around you, and fine white skin under those knickers. Ye get her going, and she'd never stop. A lot of passion packed in that bit of a body, and her hair'd be just like flame in your hands. She's got a bit of a mark on her fanny..."

"Dammit." The small, dark smile on Zach's face died. "You. *Leave her alone.*"

The instant he spoke, he felt like an idiotic fool, talking to an empty room.

Zach rolled his shoulders impatiently. It wasn't like he really believed in spooks and ghosts, but he could accept—even understand—that he was confused and exhausted right now. Left alone long enough, and anyone's mind could wander in curious directions. It seemed honestly funny... until that voice started talking about Kirstin in physically intimate detail. The ghost was a dirty old man and a voyeur to boot.

You're gonna protect her from ghosts, Zach?

You really are losing it, Connor.

With a loud exasperated sigh, Zach headed straight for the bottle of scotch.

Three

Kirstin munched on a crisp red apple as she drove to Zach's. The blacktop glistened in the watery sunlight. The snow had melted days before. This morning a typical Maine fog had shrouded the coast in fat gray clouds, but the sun had burned it off by noon.

With the apple crunched between her teeth, she glanced at her watch. Almost one. A pickup zoomed past her. Kirstin couldn't speed; her old Ford coughed and sputtered anywhere past fifty, but she waved at the other driver. Mike Josephs. She knew him. She knew almost everyone on the road at this time of year.

In the summer, the road was choked with tourist traffic, and the harbor jammed with a curious mix of fishermen's crafts and expensive sailboats. The locals called the tourists "summer complaints." Bar Harbor's economy was dependent on tourism, but that didn't mean that locals had to like it. An old joke regularly circulated about the visitor who'd said, "Sometimes I get the feeling that Mainers would be happier if we all stayed home and just mailed the money in."

Seconds later Kirstin pulled into Zach's driveway, well aware why that old joke had sprung to mind. It applied to Zach. Mainers kept their distance from outsiders, and his sleek black Lotus automatically labeled him a tourist. Unless he extended a friendly hand, he'd be left alone. No one would bother him about his hair or appearance. No one would bug him with nosy, prying, personal questions.

Unless she did.

Kirstin wrapped her apple core in a napkin, reached for her tool caddy and vaulted out of the truck. Although she'd been born and bred in Maine, something must have gone haywire in her bloodline, because she had a lot of questions about Zach. All of them nosy, prying and personal.

The front door was unlocked. She yoo-hooed, but there was no response. On the old pine table in the kitchen she found a note, succinct and to the point, "Would appreciate anything you could do with the kitchen." Two hundred dollars in twenties were attached to the note. The handwriting was a thick black scrawl.

She pulled off her jacket, studying the note, unsurprised to find her tenant gone.

Zach, she had already figured out, was painfully shy around women.

Her heart warmed, remembering their encounter five nights before. He may not have wanted her din-

ner, but he'd devoured it like a starving man after a
fast. He simply wasn't a man who accepted help easily. She understood that kind of pride.

Kirstin was quite sure he'd never intended to kiss
her, either, but there had been a moment, in the hall,
when he'd stepped toward her and raised his hand and
his searing blue eyes had lanced on her face. She'd
seen loneliness in his eyes. She'd seen need. A zillion
years ago, a stray wolf cub had wandered into her
dad's backyard, obviously hungry and cold and desperate for shelter. Her dad had put out food, but the
cub had been too scared to take it, wary of risking
anything that had a human connection. Zach reminded her of that wolf.

He had nothing to fear from her—she wasn't going
to hurt him—but it was obviously going to take some
time for him to believe that. Humming off-key, she
pushed up the sleeves of her chartreuse sweatshirt with
another glance at the table. The amount of money, of
course, was ridiculous. She'd have to settle that with
him, but for now she settled on nosing around.

The refrigerator contained a head of lettuce, a half
quart of milk, and some sandwich meat. One cupboard held a few cans of pre-made spaghetti and sim-
ilar junk food. That was it, except for coffee and a
new, unopened bottle of liquor. Brandy this time, instead of scotch.

She mentally shook her head as she peeked from
room to room. The house looked no different than it
had five days ago. He wasn't eating—at least he wasn't
eating right—and he hadn't removed any dustcovers
or aired out any of the house. Apparently he was
sleeping in the parlor, because she found a blanket and

pillow neatly stacked on the couch there. No sleeping
bag, just that one scratchy wool blanket, in spite of all
those wonderful bedrooms upstairs.

Her maternal instincts were lustily aroused. The
house needed everything. Every window washed, every
floor scrubbed, draperies freshened and furniture
polished. It couldn't be done all at once, but she could
tackle a few rooms each time. She'd do the kitchen
today, she decided, but she'd also make sure he had a
bedroom fit to sleep in.

Two hours later Zach still hadn't shown up—not
that it mattered. Humming Beethoven's Ninth, Kirstin climbed the stairs, juggling her tool caddy and an
armload of sheets still hot from the dryer. The hall
upstairs was long enough to bowl in, dark and dim,
with a priceless chestnut floor that had been crimi-
nally neglected for years, but that would wait. There
were six bedrooms and two baths off the hall. She
knew which one she wanted.

The master bedroom was really something. French
doors led to an open porch, with a winsomely romantic view of the deserted lighthouse and the pounding
Atlantic. A gigantic four-poster bed dominated the
room, teak, mounted on a box pedestal. A woman
could get lost in that bed with the right man, Kirstin
thought wickedly, and the thick feather mattress was
big enough to drown in.

The Persian rug was old, but still plush, still cush-
iony deep. An antique quilted dressing stand stood in
one corner, with a floor-length gilded mirror behind
it. Kirstin could easily imagine a woman undressing
behind that stand, with her lover impatiently waiting.
She pulled off more dust sheets, finding a red bro-

cade lounging chaise, a tall chiffonier ornately carved in zebra wood and a throne-style chair with claw feet upholstered in rich, wine-red velvet.

She paused for a moment, not that she needed the rest. She just wanted to look. For all the old houses she'd worked in, none had a sexier bedroom than this one. It was a room of sybaritic luxury, full of textures and sensual comforts. It made her think of pirates and captive princesses, of wedding nights and virgins, of wild winds and moonlight and lovers caught up in uncontrollably fierce passion....

A sudden draft feathered over her skin. Behind her, the bedroom door closed. She whirled around in surprise, nearly bumping her shin on the edge of the chaise. Crossing the room, she twisted the doorknob.

It was locked. Perplexed, she rattled it hard. A waste of time, the knob wouldn't budge.

She seemed to be locked in.

Kirstin stepped back, vaguely remembering the front door "mysteriously" locking when she'd come over on Thanksgiving. Her lips twitched. Zach had to have done that. Who else? She doubted he'd meant to do it; it was more like the unconscious gesture of a man who was too shy, too proud, to admit he wanted and needed some company.

The darling was terribly lonely. Possibly lonelier than he realized himself. Being locked in his bedroom, though, was a tad embarassing. It wasn't as if she were trapped; there were stairs off the porch balcony outside, but hopefully she wouldn't need to use them. It was bitter cold out, and her jacket was downstairs. Zach surely didn't intend to take his little joke that far.

"Zach?" she called out. *"Zach?"*

Zach was frozen to the bone. With a glance at his watch, he saw it was finally five.

She had to be gone from the house by now.

His legs were cramped as he lurched to his feet. He'd found a sheltered spot to sit, a saucer-shaped cove in the lee of the wind, but the cold had long seeped through his limbs. His hair and face felt crusted with salt spray; his feet were nearly numb. The sun had dropped, the sky turned the murky dark of dusk. The water was ruffled with the dance of gray diamonds, and even the gulls had disappeared. The rocks were slick and slippery, harder to climb down than up. He didn't really care.

His mind was on Sylvie. Had been all afternoon. Like a toddler who couldn't resist picking at a scab, Zach kept seeing her face. Sylvie, of the coal-black hair and flashing, sparkling eyes.

It had been late, the night he met her. Past midnight, after a gig; he'd been exhausted, but still pumping an adrenaline high from the power of the music. It wasn't often he felt that thrill anymore. As a teenager, the hot lights and swell of applause and big crowds had been a kick, but lately he'd felt impatient, restless, weary of living in the limelight. That night, though, he'd forgotten the crowd, forgotten everything but the music. The band had always played a mixture of rock and blues, but that night they concentrated on blues, his favorite, and the music had just come, pouring out of him as if he'd opened a hot pulsing vein. It was one of those rare times when he could do no wrong, when every note and chord was perfect. The beat was smoky and sexy and primitive and came straight from his soul. He forgot the audience was even there until they'd start screaming and chanting for an encore.

Later, Sylvie had found him in the bar with the rest of the band. From the way she walked, the way she moved, Zach knew she was on the prowl. She separated him from the pack as efficiently as a she-panther who'd chosen her prey. He'd liked the rush, been amused, and she'd been damn beautiful. Her boyfriend had taken off after a seven-year-long relationship, she'd told him, and she was lonely. Very lonely.

Zach hadn't suckered into a one-night stand in years. The women who pursued him on the road didn't really want him. They wanted the charge of bedding down with a rock star. He had no illusions that Sylvie was different, but he just didn't want to be alone that night. The band had been on the road for months, either sacking out in the Bluebird or motel rooms, and he was weary of waking up alone. She wanted him. It was enough. He had protection, but never used it because she had a diaphram. At the time, he wasn't thinking about the percentages of chance with that particular device. She'd been insatiable and hot and she'd worn him out. Surprising him not at all, though, she'd disappeared before he woke up in the morning.

Zach leaped off the last rock onto level ground. Shoving his hands into his pockets, he headed up the yard for the house. Sylvie had wanted the spice of some kinky sex with a rock star. She'd used him. No differently than he'd used her, to chase away the loneliness. At the time he hadn't seen anything wrong with it. They were both consenting adults, neither hurt by the encounter.

And he'd believed that, until she called up three months later. Tracked him down from Michigan, to tell him that she was pregnant. And that she wanted money.

Clamping his jaw, Zach forced the memories away. Reliving his encounters with lawyers and the final ugly trick Sylvie had played on him did no good. It was that night that mattered. That night echoed everything he'd become—a careless, selfish, self-centered bastard who never thought twice about sleeping with a woman he barely knew. And because of what he'd become, a baby had been made. A baby that was part of his blood, his genes, his soul. *His* baby. A baby who was being raised by strangers instead of him, and he'd never even know, dammit, if she was loved.

Nothing was changeable now. The end of the story was written in stone. The only thing he'd ever had power over was the beginning. He'd have sold his soul to take back that one night.

The price on his soul—the unlivable weight load of a price—was that he couldn't.

Head down, Zach pushed open the back door and kicked off his damp boots. His temples were throbbing with a familiar headache, and his feet were frozen. With enough brandy, maybe he could freeze the voice of his conscience.

He crossed the kitchen and fumbled in the cupboard for a glass, vaguely aware that the room smelled different, looked different. Pine and bleach. Fresh, clean smells, like his mother's kitchen a million years ago. He twisted the top off the brandy, and then went dead still.

"Zach? *Zach?*"

No, he assured himself. She couldn't still be here.

Unfortunately when he pressed his nose to the window, Kirstin's rattrap of a pickup—how could he have missed seeing it?—was still parked in the driveway.

"Zach?"

He heard her, he heard her. But coming from where? When she called again, he realized the confounded woman was somewhere upstairs.

He took the steps two at a time, but then stopped, confused, at the shadowed dark landing. There were a half-dozen doors, all closed. He groped for a light switch, but didn't find one. "Where are you?"

"Come on, Zach. You know very well where I am!"

That was hardly true, but the sound of her voice led him to the right door. The key was right in the lock. All he had to do was turn it. Seconds before, he could have sworn that nothing could distract him from the bleak, morose thoughts in his mind.

But she did.

Kirstin's eyes homed to his like an arrow for a target. Her white skin was flushed, her hair tumbling around a black hairband. She was wearing work clothes, just a sweatshirt and jeans, but the sweatshirt was a screaming-bright green with Mellie's Mom spelled out in the whimsically spangled arc of a rainbow.

"You all right?" A stupid question; he could see she was all right. From her clothes to her expression, she looked like she always did—an honest-to-pete good woman, a believer in rainbows, kids and the intrinsic goodness of mankind. The kind of woman, Zach reminded himself, who could never understand the kinds of mistakes he'd made. He raked a hand through his hair. "How on *earth* did you get locked in here?"

"You know how," she said with wry humor, and then more softly, "It's all right, Zach. I understand. It was a joke. It was just that I started to worry when you didn't come right away."

So far, Zach had yet to be able to anticipate what was going to come out of her mouth, but she truly befuddled him this time. He started to respond, then couldn't. She seemed to be under the insane assumption that he would deliberately have locked her in. That was nuts. Beyond nuts. But damned if he could explain how doors kept mysteriously locking when she was around . . . without mentioning ghosts and sounding nuts himself.

"It's okay," she repeated reassuringly. With a winsome, warm smile, she motioned to the room. "I didn't mind being stuck up here. There was lots to do. I threw some sheets in the wash while I was doing the kitchen. You surely didn't want to keep sleeping downstairs, but the bedroom really needed a clean and polish to make it livable. I don't know if you realized what was under all the dustcovers—"

He had no idea what was under all the dustcovers. He hadn't been up here. Now he looked past her, to the den-of-iniquity of a bedroom. Red velvet. Brocade. Persian rugs. A bed big enough for a bachelor with a harem. And Kirstin standing there, with apple color streaking up her cheeks when she realized she'd drawn attention to that big, wide feather mattress.

Her gaze whisked to his face, then quickly away. It didn't take a mind reader for Zach to guess that she thought he'd had a teensy, subtle ulterior motive for locking her specifically here. In a bedroom. Near that big, wide, empty bed.

He opened his mouth for a second time. Not a damn thing came out. If his life depended on it, he wasn't positive if he could come up with anything to say.

Kirstin, dependably, never suffered from that problem. "There was an article about you in the paper on Sunday," she rushed on. "At least, I think it was about you. AP, not local, and there weren't any pictures. But the article was about the breakup of a band named Streak of Fire. Zachary Connor, it said, was the lead and songwriter. You?"

"Yeah." Damn, he thought. The news had to come out. They'd canceled concerts. But once the legal breakup of the band hit the newspapers, both his brothers would be on his tail to find out what happened. And he wasn't sure he could tell them.

"So. You played . . . rock?"

"The band was pretty eclectic. Some rock, some rhythm and blues."

"And your field is music?"

"Not anymore," he said curtly. She'd had the good sense to move away from the bed. He watched her whisking around the room, gathering up different supplies. A plastic tool case lay open on the carpet, stuffed with everything from screwdrivers to rags to cleaning products. Her jeans had a hole in one knee. The bridge of her nose had a smattering of freckles.

If there was a woman born who was less like Sylvie—or all the Sylvies in his life—it had to be her. Zach knew how to behave around women who were users and takers. They were like him. Kirstin was as fresh and wholesome as a spring breeze. Clean, like sunlight. And a walking disaster to his peace of mind.

She'd put the idea in his head. Of them. In that bed. In the dark, the moonlight glowing through the French doors, her hair a fire of curls against the crisp white pillow, that long skinny body wrapped around him in the night.

"I like music," Kirstin said with a cheeky grin, "but it never seemed to like me. Dancing . . . I was always a klutz. And I tried out for clarinet in fifth grade, but didn't last a day. The music teacher begged me to take art. My dad isn't bad with a fiddle, and Mellie has a terrific little voice, but heaven knows she didn't inherit the talent from me. Is this rest of your family musical?"

Restlessly Zach shifted in the doorway. She was making wholesome chitchat and he was imagining her naked. *You are not a nice man, Zach Connor.* As if that were news. "No," he answered her, "that kind of insanity thankfully doesn't run in the family. Both my brothers were born practical. As fast as Michael was out of knee pants, he was in oxford button-downs. He started with a watered-down lemonade stand at age nine, and has been making money ever since. Seth . . . he always puttered with his hands. He's a carpenter, and a good one. Fancy cabinetwork, that kind of thing."

"I'll bet Seth would like some of the antiques in this house?"

"Yeah, he would."

"How about the rest of your family?" Kirstin stuck a bottle of window cleaner and the roll of paper towels into the tool caddy.

"There's just my dad. Mom split when we were all young, and Dad—he never even thought about remarrying again. It ended up just us. A household of men. None of the Connor men are exactly known for luck with women."

"Neither of your brothers are married?"

"Just Michael."

Kirstin latched the toolbox and glanced up. "There's something in your voice. I take it you don't like his wife?"

Zach rubbed the back of his neck. "He thinks the sun rises and sets on her. I guess she's all right. Carla's just the kind who always looks just right, acts just right...like she doesn't have to spit after brushing her teeth like everybody else. I've never seen her with a hair out of place. Michael—he's more real than that. I never understood how the two of them could be happy...." His voice trailed off. He'd never meant to run on. He never talked personally about himself or his family, not with strangers, not with anyone.

Kirstin was finished with the room. If she noticed the sudden silence, for once she didn't seem compelled to fill it. Night had come on. When she flicked off the overhead light, the room flooded with charcoal-fuzzy shadows.

"I'll carry that case of yours downstairs." He'd seen the conglomerate weight of stuff she'd packed into it.

"Thanks. It's heavy." Yet ignoring the tool caddy altogether, she walked straight toward him. Quietly. Purposefully. "Zach, I have to leave. My family's likely to call out the troopers if I don't get home soon. I'm never this late. But I just want to tell you...if you want a friend, you've got one."

Maybe he could have stopped her, if he'd just anticipated what she was going to do. Both his hands were jammed into his jeans pockets when she reached up. Her fingertips touched his bearded jaw. Her palm slid to his cheek, her touch as light as a tickle, then trailed further to cup his head. Reddish-pale lashes webbed her cheeks when she closed her eyes. And then she raised up on tiptoe and kissed him.

He froze. She meant an expression of affection, he guessed. Nothing complicated, nothing heavy, just something to illustrate her offer to be friends. It'd be over faster than a finger snap if he had the good sense to stand there as still as a dead fish.

She lifted her head. Instead of moving away, though, she didn't move at all. Her eyes opened, lustrous, luminous, softer and deeper than the blue of a lake. The teensiest frown perched on her brow. The friendly peck had been short. Long enough to arouse her feminine curiosity, but apparently too short to appease it. Zach knew damn well she was coming after another.

He yanked his hands out of his pockets, thinking hell, she belonged behind a locked gate with a dozen trained Dobermans. For a woman who claimed to have been married, he couldn't fathom how she'd developed so little judgment about men. He wasn't a man she should trust, wasn't a man she should even be thinking about fooling around with, and he intended to push her away. Roughly if he had to. And snapping out a clear-cut rejection, if he had to do that.

He opened his mouth...too late. Her lips were already brushing his again, luringly, invitingly. He latched his hands around her waist, repressively tight, but somehow he didn't push her away as he meant to. He just didn't know how to reject her without hurting her feelings. How the hell was he supposed to hurt a woman who wore rainbows on her sweatshirt and still had stars in her eyes? And she totally confused him when she murmured something in the darkness, not specific words, but just a whispered sound communicating reassurance. To him. As if she thought *he* needed reassurance. The pad of her thumb discovered the deep grove crease in his brow; she smoothed the crease with a woman's gesture older than time. It's okay, Zach, she seemed to be telling him. Just take it easy. Everything's okay.

But nothing was suddenly okay. Nothing was suddenly easy. He told himself that every man was attracted to the one woman he couldn't have. Kirstin was forbidden fruit. The one woman on earth he should have the conscience, the character, to leave alone.

But her mouth rubbed against his, supple and yielding and dangerously distracting. She tasted like peppermint, as if she'd had a piece of candy not long ago, and the spice still lingered on her lips. Beneath that was just her, the unique flavor of Kirstin, wild and dark and hopelessly sweet.

He'd kissed a hundred women. None like her. In his world, a kiss was a complicated prelude to sex, a test of his adequacy and performance. He understood women who wanted something from him. Kirstin seemed to want nothing at all. Her kiss was a gift, her mouth an offering. He'd been alone so long, and she was there. He'd been cold, on the inside, for as far back as he could remember, and her lips stroked his, as light and warm as the caress of sunlight. Her touch was careful, as if she were under the insane illusion that he could break. Gentle, as if she were under the equally insane illusion that the slightest pressure could hurt him.

She was the vulnerable one. Not him. And when he angled his head and deepened the kiss, he promised himself that he'd let her go. Next to her, he felt old, stained, jaded, darkened by sins and mistakes that she'd never understand, and the right thing to do was leave her alone. And he would. In a minute.

At that precise instant, he was too scared to let her go. Something crazy was happening. Something impossible. Something he could make no sense of, and it was all linked to her.

Her right hand had drifted to his neck, curled in the collar of his shirt and clung. Her lips parted, responsive to the pressure of his, and her whole body swayed closer, igniting an arousal that made his blood run thick. Her tongue tasted sweeter than any sugar. He could feel the warmth of her skin beneath the heavy sweatshirt, the tightening of her small breasts against his chest. More, he could feel the sudden beat of her nerves in the darkness. Feminine nerves, aware of him now, aware of desire, of need. She was talking to him, with the beat of her heart, with the primitive thud of her pulse. And he heard her. That's what made no sense. Because it was music he heard, the blues of an achingly lonely love song, mystical magical notes that seemed to be playing from her heart to his.

He jerked his head back, abruptly feeling shaken and stupid and foolish. The silence in the dark, empty bedroom was a quick slam of reality. There was no music. It was just something about Kirstin that... confused him. The confounded woman had been confusing him from the day he met her.

She let out her breath in a silky little rush and raised her eyes, meeting his. Her arms were still laced around his neck. She lowered them slowly, her gaze on his face dreamily bemused.

"No one," she murmured, "ever kissed me like that."

He didn't want to hear that. Even a lamb should have more sense than to admit her vulnerability to a wolf. Guilt pummeled through him. He should never have touched her. He'd *known* he had no right to touch her. "Nothing happened," he said sharply.

"Maybe not for you." Her smile was soft, teasing.

He was briefly inclined to tear his hair out by the roots. "Kirstin," he said patiently, "we're alone in this house. When a guy comes on to you, that you don't know from Adam, in a place where you could shout from here to Atlanta and never be heard, you're supposed to knock his block off."

"Yeah?"

"Yeah."

"I'll remember that next time," she murmured.

"There won't be a next time."

"Okay, Zach." She smiled again. And then she was gone.

Four

Fifteen minutes later, Zach was still standing in the dark, his hands deep in his pockets and his mood... edgy. The roar of the ocean filtered through the French doors. Shadows, darker than lead, played on the tall pedestal bed. It was a bedroom that could make a monk think of sex, and that, he decided, was the problem. The right atmosphere, after a long period of abstinence, had simply triggered some basic biological hormones.

He had *not* heard music with Kirstin. The idea was ridiculous. And he certainly hadn't shared something rare and special with her. That idea was even more rattling.

Abruptly he turned on his heel. Thankfully there was an extremely simple way to prove that those no-tions were nonsense. He whipped out of the room and headed down the hall.

A chill draft caught up with him on the stairs, as familiar as a relentless hound nipping at his heels. "You must have done something right, lad. Her cheeks were all aflush, her eyes as shiny as jewels. She near killed herself, tripping down the steps outside. Kissed her, did ye?"

"You ought to know." As of 2:00 a.m. that morning, he'd started talking back to the ghost. Another sign of lunacy, Zach thought dryly. But it was just because he was alone. And the endless silence in the old house had been unbearable in the dark hours of the night.

"Well, now, truthfully I don't know what ye did with the lass. I have the run of the house, but not the master bedroom. Can't see through the doorway, never could, but that doesn't mean I can't help ye, lad, should you need a teensy bit of instruction. I've bedded dozens in my time. Learned from a master of lovers, Teach, Edward Teach. You surely had some history in your schooling? They called him Blackbeard back then, and I'll tell you, there was nothing Teach didn't know about women...."

"Hmm." Zach was willing to tolerate these imaginary conversations. They filled a void. Who cared if they were lunatic or not? Nobody'd ever know. But just then, his mind was focused elsewhere.

"...I didn't tell ye, lad, but I was hung in my time. Hung for piracy, long after they caught Teach on the Carolina Coast. Black crimes they accused me of, and I have to say I was guilty of every one of them. But loving, lad, I was good at love. Never harmed a woman. Never met a woman I couldn't love, though a few, mind ye, were easier to love in the dark. In my time, so many had bad teeth and pock scars—"

"Maybe we could have this conversation later, Jock." Flipping on lights, he aimed straight for the octagonal-shaped turret room.

"—well, anyhoo, it's my charge, for those living in the house, to find them a true love. It's not like we have a choice. We're in this together, we are, and there's no point in yer bein' so surly, lad, when I can be of enormous help to ye. Ye clearly made a good start with that kiss, but I couldna help but notice that she still had all her clothes on—"

"You start looking under her clothes again, and I swear I'll hire an exorcist. You hear me, Jock? Leave Kirstin *alone*." Zach entered the room and kicked the door closed. He took a long breath.

There were no ghosts in here. There was nothing at all, except for his keyboard and the case for his sax in the middle of the dusty parquet floor. He didn't bother turning on the light because he didn't need it to know what he was doing. Hunching down, he snapped the catch on the case and cradled the sax. In seconds he'd slid on the mouthpiece; the neckpiece had to be snapped in, then screwed on. He could have done it in his sleep.

When he stood up, the weight of the instrument lay between his legs as intimately as a lover. She'd been his lover once. She was the only way he'd ever known how to communicate the things that really mattered. The keyboard was the more versatile instrument, easier for composing, good for any kind of music from classical to rock to country, but it wasn't as good for blues. His sax was made for blues.

A lot of people associated the blues with sadness, but that was the only the tiny tip of the iceberg. Zach had spent long hours studying it. It was a music created by slaves in a time when they could not, dare not, communicate with language, so they'd found another way to express emotion. One instrument called, the other responded. The soul of blues was vocal, that call and response pattern a way of talking without words, a way to express tears, joy, love, grief, pain, elation. Zach had never talked easily. Not about feelings. The sax had always done it for him—poured out all those things that a man couldn't say. Closing his eyes, he bit down on the mouthpiece and willed his old lover to talk to him.

For a half hour he tried. Then another half hour.

It just wouldn't come. Like a rat trapped in a cage, he craved the release, and the right fingers on the right keys should have opened the door. It wasn't as if he'd forgotten how to play, as if there was anything missing in his technical expertise. Every note came out true. But stringing notes and chords together wasn't enough to make music, not the kind of music that meant anything.

Zach rolled back his head, the instrument still nestled in his hands. He'd heard something with Kirstin. Or he thought he had. The timbre and pulse of notes he'd never heard before. The low, silky beat of a love song, the chords fresh, pure, powerful, like nothing he'd done before, nothing he knew. For a moment, with her, the music had been so real he could have touched it.

It was gone without her. He couldn't get it back. Hell, maybe he'd imagined it. Imagined the song, just as he'd imagined that unique, intimate connection with Kirstin.

Impatiently he detached the mouth and neck pieces and laid the sax back in its case. An image of a wide fragile mouth and a frizzy mop of red-brown hair was burned in his brain. She reminded him of backyard barbecues and a decked-out Christmas tree and blueberry pie. She was clean, clean on the inside, too giving and honest for her own good, and damnation, she'd given away the farm when she kissed. Who would have guessed she had all that gunpowder and fire hidden under those wholesome freckles? How could he have known she'd come alive in his arms like a power-packed concentration of TNT? She could take a man under with all that passion and promise, make a man believe he was needed and wanted and incomparably special to her.

Stay away from her, growled his conscience.

As if he needed the warning. Zach stared bleakly into the black night. Damn, he knew why he'd let her broadside him. It was a sweet respite from hell, her thinking he was a good guy, someone worth knowing, worth caring about. For a man battling with self-respect, she was an incredibly powerful intoxicant. But Zach suspected it wouldn't take much to extinguish that soft, vulnerable look in her eyes. The truth would do it. It didn't take a 200 IQ to figure out how Kirstin felt about family and commitments and kids. Especially kids. She'd never understand a man who would carelessly risk a child.

Hell, neither could he. He had yet to find a way to live with the sin on his conscience, but resolving the problem of Kirstin was far easier. There'd be no more kisses, no more clinches. There couldn't be, if Zach kept a five-mile distance between them. From now on, he intended to be completely out of sight when she was around. And that was a guarantee.

Kirstin was tingling with anticipation as she turned into Zach's driveway. She was two hours early, but surely he wouldn't mind. Coming early today simply made good sense. The sky was already spitting snow and sleet, and the forecast for the coming night was a squaller of a snowstorm. She wanted to be done and back home before the truly bad weather hit, especially because Mellie was with her.

"Okay, punkin." Kirstin braked and turned the key, then leaned over to unsnap Mellie from the seat belt. There'd been no school today because of teachers' conferences. Her daughter was as antsy as a caged monkey. "Remember what I told you?"

"Yup. I'm gonna be as quiet as a mouse. Mr. Connor knows I come with you to work sometimes, but we don't want to be in his way." Mollie mounded her arms with Mercer Mayer books, markers, Moose, two dolls and a baby bottle. Surely, Kirstin thought, enough to keep her occupied.

"Right. Now it's slippery, so we're going to walk slowly, slooowwwllly, to the front porch so we don't slip and fall, okay?" Kirstin waited until Mellie nodded dutifully. Then watched, with a sigh, as her daughter bounded out of the truck and galloped like

a pony to the front door. There was no containing
Mellie's exuberant energy today.

She couldn't move as quickly herself. Too much to
carry. The wind snatched her parka hood. Icy rain attacked her bare head as she tried to juggle her tool
caddy of supplies with her purse, a covered tuna casserole and a still warm blueberry pie. The resulting pile
was precariously balanced and heavier than stone.
When she swung a hip to close the truck door, the pie
tin dangerously teetered.

Her heart felt just as teetery at the thought of seeing Zach again. He had to be home. He couldn't possibly be out walking in this weather.

Their embrace still lingered in her mind, stuck there
like the stinger from a bee. She just couldn't seem to
forget it. She'd sensed he was troubled and lonely, but
not how troubled, how lonely, until he'd wrapped his
arms around her. His heart, God, his heart had been
beating so hard. He'd held on as if she was the only
life buoy in the ocean, and no man had ever kissed her
that way. Fiercely. Wickedly. Even . . . roughly. When
he'd finally let her go, she'd felt dizzy and trembling
and embarassingly flush-hot from her toes to her fingertips.

Alan, always, had made her feel wanted. But not
like that. She'd never ignited that kind of raw sexual-
ity or hunger in any man . . . although Kirstin thought
she understood what happened. It wasn't necessarily
her. He'd told her that his field was music. She had
immediately pictured a life-style of constant travel-
ing, motel rooms, late nights and strangers. A horri-
bly lonely life. It was really no wonder that he was
desperate for human contact.

Snow spitting in her face, arms aching from her awkward, heavy load, Kirstin edged up the slippery walk toward the door. Truthfully she was a teensy bit appalled at her shameless response to him. It was hardly appropriate behavior for a responsible, practical single mom. But she suspected that Zach was feeling even more shy than she was after that encounter. He was clearly unsure around women, and men never easily exposed emotions that way. It would be up to her to make sure he wasn't embarassed. She'd be calm and cool about it. Natural. The image of a poised, mature, adult woman friend.

"Mellie, can you get the door, punkin? Mommie's hands are full."

"Mom, I *can't*. I'll drop Moose."

"Okay, okay." Well, Kirstin thought humorously, it wasn't strictly *okay*. There was no question that she could get in. Even if Zach wasn't home, she had her caretaker's key. To even try the door, though, required a free hand.

The blueberry pie was on top, balanced on the glass lid of the casserole. The glass top jiggled noisily, threatening to tip, the instant she tried to move. No good. Balancing her chin on top of the pie tin, the pile seemed reasonably secure. Carefully she bent down and fumbled for the doorknob.

The door popped open. Fast. So fast that her mind didn't immediately register that Zach must have responded to the sound of footsteps on his porch. She didn't immediately see Zach at all. When she stumbled in, the tuna-fish casserole skidded and slid, and the pie...oh, God, the pie was airborne. And sailing straight for a solid white sweatshirt.

"Hi, Mr. Connor. You remember me, don't you? I'm Mellie, and I'm going to be very quiet today."

Like a slow motion horror show, Kirstin heard Mellie's innocently cheerful voice, saw Zach's shocked blue eyes when the pie connected with his chest. "Oh, God. Oh, God." With rattling speed, she dropped the toolbox and her purse and plopped the casserole on the floor. Zach's hands had instinctively shot out to catch the pie. And he'd caught it. But not before it tipped, and even wrapped carefully in tinfoil, blueberries splattered all over him. "What have I done? I'm so sorry, Zach. I think I'm going to die." She had fresh cleaning rags somewhere. She always had rags. Only darn it, *where?* "I did a little cooking and baking this morning. I just thought you might like something home baked. The weather was so bad...that's why we're early, and oh, Lord, I'm never going to be able to get blueberry stains out of that white sweatshirt..." She found a rag. There was a blotch of blue right at his ribs. She dabbed at it frantically. Another blotch was dribbling down the hem of his sweatshirt to his jeans. She aimed lower. "Just shoot me, okay? It's the only way I'm going to feel better—"

"Ah...Kirstin?"

"—Just once, just once in my whole life, I'd like to be graceful. I'll clean this all up. You don't have to worry about a thing—"

"Kirstin."

Something in his voice made her head shoot up. Something in his eyes made her head shoot instantly back down. Abruptly she realized where she'd been rubbing the rag. Directly over his zipper. Over the distinctly growing masculine bulge in his zipper. She

promptly dropped the rag. A flush climbed her cheeks
as hot as a burn.

"Oh, my. Oh, dear. I didn't mean to...um—"

"I *know* what you didn't mean to do. Just calm
down, okay? Everything's fine. Nothing to worry
about."

But there was something to worry about, she
thought. She'd never seen him laugh before, and
though the curve of his lips hardly qualified as a full-
fledged chuckle, it was close. Maybe he didn't want to
find the situation comical, but he did. The sparkle of
life and humor in his face transformed his stark features, erased the driven, harsh lines around his eyes.
When was the last time he'd had the chance to be a
mischievous boy? She'd neither noticed nor cared if he
was good-looking before, still didn't, but darned if he
didn't take her breath away.

For a moment, anyway. Belatedly she noticed that
Zach was holding the pie in midair, as if his only sure
way of protecting it was keeping it far above her reach.

"Heaven knows what shape it's in now, but I'll take
it in the kitchen—"

"Now, don't take offense, Kirstin, but I think it'd
be safer if I did."

"You aren't kidding, Mr. Connor," Mellie piped in.

It was the first instant Zach had had to really notice Mellie. Kirstin watched his head turn. She hadn't
forgotten her embarassment over the disastrous mess
she'd made, but for the breath of a second, time sus-
pended. Zach seemed to freeze when he looked at
Mellie. She saw his expression change. The boyish grin
disappeared and his jaw tightened. His eyes darkened
with a softness as deep as pain.

And then he stiffened, straighter than a ramrod. "I should have known this wouldn't work," he murmured, half to himself. And then to her he said, "Kirstin, could I talk to you for a second in the kitchen?"

"What isn't going to work?" She snatched up the casserole and trailed after him, feeling both bewildered and concerned by his sudden change in mood.

"You being here. This arrangement. I..." He set the pie on the counter, and waited until she'd set down the glass casserole dish. In the dimly lit kitchen, it was hard to see his expression, but he was obviously grappling for the right words to say. "It didn't occur to me before that this whole arrangement was unfair to you. You're a caretaker. Not a housecleaner. It was pretty damn sexist of me to just assume this was work you usually do. And it's not like I'm some chauvinistic jerk who's incapable of washing his own floors. I just think it would be more fair to you if we called this whole thing off."

It was sweet, his worrying about being "fair to her." But Kirstin would have bet her last dollar that he was worried about something else entirely. "Well, it's true that I don't usually clean houses," she agreed slowly, watching his eyes. "Handyman stuff is usually my thing. Security systems. The kind of fix-its and problems that happen in empty houses, that absentee owners need someone to take care of."

"That's what I figured—"

She gently interrupted him. "But I volunteered for this work, remember? I'm crazy about this house, always have been. Cleaning it up is like a chance to make it come alive again. And I never thought you were a chauvinist, looking for a maid to pick up after him. The house is huge. How could you possibly do it all yourself? Especially if you only have a month to be here."

She saw him hesitate. He didn't try denying that he needed the help, so that wasn't what was really bothering him. It had to be something about Mellie, she thought. It was when he'd looked at her Amelia Anne that he'd suddenly become all shook up.

"Does being around children bother you?" she asked quietly. "Originally you said it was all right if I occasionally brought Mellie. Most of the time my dad's around for the few hours she's home after school, but if it's a problem for you—"

"Of course you can bring her. It's not a problem."

"Hmm. Well, I can't blame you for being aggravated about the pie. But if I promise not to throw any more pies at you..." She hoped to coax another smile, but it wasn't to be.

"Kirstin, I don't give a royal damn about the pie."

She nodded thoughtfully. Whatever was troubling him, he didn't seem willing to tell her. She understood. He hardly knew her well enough to trust her— at least not yet. "Okay. I'm going to get to work. I brought change from the money you left me last time, but when I'm done, I'll just leave it on the kitchen table. You don't have to worry if you need some peace and quiet, Zach. It's a big house—you won't even know we're here," she promised.

Not know she was there? What a joke.

Noisy sleet pelted on the windows in the library. The weather wasn't fit for dogs. The best he could do was find a place to hide out, and when Kirstin and the kid went upstairs, the library struck him as a reasonably safe sanctuary.

He squished the button on the cleaning spray. It was his first experience washing windows. His arms already ached, his fingers were sore and a lack-of-sleep headache was throbbing in his temples. It couldn't be helped. He couldn't sleep now, not with her in the house. And where he grew up, no man sat around like a lazy hound when a woman was working. He unraveled some sheets of paper towels and started rubbing.

Unfortunately the more he rubbed, the more he was reminded of the way she'd tried to rub the blueberry stains off the front of his jeans. He'd almost laughed at the startled look of shock in her eyes when she realized he was aroused. His reaction to being rubbed had been automatic, unavoidable biology. She surely knew that. So did he. Only that excuse was long gone, and his hormones were still bucking in overdrive.

Maybe she'd been put on this earth to drive him insane, he considered seriously. All he wanted from life was peace and quiet. Instead, he got ghosts and her. Especially her. She made him laugh, made him feel alive again. He couldn't understand it. She had freckles, for heaven's sakes. Hair that looked like she'd plugged into an electric socket. She was a truly disastrous klutz, the least restful woman he'd ever met and she even wore clothes loud enough to wake the dead. She was the one woman who could never be part of his life, so why couldn't he get her off his mind?

A muted, distant sound made his head jerk up. What *now?* The barely audible sound had a remarkable resemblance to discordant musical chords, as if a mouse had run over his electric keyboard. Perplexed, he popped the library door open and strode down the hall toward the turret room, twisted the doorknob, poked his head in . . . and abruptly stopped.

Mellie had been upstairs with Kirstin for the past half hour, but apparently she'd escaped her mother's watchful eyes. She was sitting cross-legged on the floor. She'd opened his sax case. His cords and reeds and swabs were scattered around, and she'd clearly figured out how to plug in his keyboard. The miniature maestro wore purple socks scuffed over her white sneakers and a pink sweatshirt with big purple fluff-balls all over the place. Her black curly hair was standing up in cowlicky spikes.

It hurt Zach to look at her. Hurt like a rusty blade sawing at his heart. It was just accidental that she had black curly hair, like his, blue eyes, like his. The similarities were just a twist of fate, but knowing that didn't help. Every time he saw her he pictured the daughter he'd never see, the daughter he'd never know.

He didn't want to look at her. He didn't want to be in the same room with her. It was nothing personal. He just wanted to be on the other side of the moon. And he'd have tried to disappear that far, that fast, if she didn't suddenly lift her bright blue eyes and spot him in the doorway.

"Oh, gosh. I shouldn't have touched this stuff without asking, right?"

"Right."

"I don't think my mom heard me. She's way on the other side of the upstairs. But I'll be dead meat if you tell her I was messing with your stuff," she admitted dolefully.

He wasn't charmed, Zach told himself. It was just that he didn't want to be responsible for Kirstin having to scold her. "I didn't say I was going to tell your mom."

"Well, that's a relief. She's told me a hundred zillion times not to touch other people's stuff without asking. But sometimes I just can't seem to help myself. I get so curious I can't *stand* it. You're not mad at me, are you?"

"No," Zach said shortly. He bent down to scoop up the corks and reeds.

"Is all this music stuff yours?"

"Yeah."

"Both things? The little piano and the gold thing?"

"The gold thing is called a saxophone. And, yes, they're both mine."

"My whole life, my whole entire life, I wanted to make music," she announced gravely. When this produced no response, she tried again. "Do you know how to play, Mr. Connor?"

"I know how."

"Could you make some music for me?"

Now there was a question straight from hell, Zach thought dryly. He'd promised himself that morning to stay away from the instruments from now on. Trying to play was only an exercise in self-torture. Both female Gramses had the instinctive gift for pouring salt into open sores. The daughter wasn't as bad as the mother, but it was a close race. The kid was the picture of his worst nightmare, and the "daymare" that haunted his waking hours was the loss of his music.

"Please, Mr. Connor?" Mellie persisted. In a blink she bounced up and skipped over to trustingly grab his hand. "If you can't play good, it's okay. I can't play good, either. You know the Christmas song about better watch out, better not shout, don't you? *Everyone* knows that song. I mean, you could play something real easy like that."

Her small stubby hand looked swallowed in his. He wanted to yank away from the contact. He wanted to snap at her to stay out of his way, leave him alone and, no, he wasn't going to "make her any music." But there was no way he could have done any of those things without hurting her feelings or making her feel bad. He couldn't hurt the kid. He'd have swallowed arsenic before hurting any child, and dammit, those bright blue eyes were pleading with him.

"I'll make you a deal," he said gruffly. "I'll play you one song and that's it. After that, we put the instruments away. You can play in the other rooms in the house, but not this one. That's the deal."

"That would be a terrific deal," Mellie assured him. "I won't ask you again. Cross my heart and hope to die. May rats eat me. May Mrs. Melroy keep me after school for the rest of my life. I would even eat squash. *That's* how big a promise I'm making you."

"I'm impressed. But all I'm asking is that you stick to the terms."

"Okeydoke."

Too late, he discovered that he'd failed to firm up the fine points of the verbal contract. As soon as he settled on the floor, the urchin seemed to blithely assume that he wanted her on his lap. She thunked down between his legs with a grin bigger than the sky and as hopelessly happy as her mother's. Her little body was warmer than a furnace; she couldn't sit still to save her life, and the damn kid was a welcher.

He played the Santa Claus tune. She ruthlessly begged for another. He played a nursery rhyme. She begged for another. How could a seven-year-old kid with grubby hands have the seductive eyes of an enchantress? The brat had suckered him into a third tune when he suddenly realized Kirstin was standing in the doorway.

Her arms were folded over her chest, her head resting against the doorjamb, her eyes glowing, like the soft warmth of a bed of embers, on the two of them together.

Mellie noticed she was there. "Hi, Moms."

"Hi, punkin. Lovebug, I told you we weren't going to bother Mr. Connor."

"It's Zach, Mom. He says he's sick of being called Mr. Connor. And Zach loves me. I wasn't bothering him. Just ask him."

Zach opened his mouth to defend himself against this incredibly unfounded accusation, but Kirstin responded before he had to. She smoothly promised him total peace and quiet—again—and took off with the kid back upstairs.

He believed her. God had surely given him his quota of impossible trials today. Nothing else could happen. He was sure of it. It was quiet downstairs—even restful—for a whole half hour.

Until he heard a startled feminine shriek echoing from upstairs.

Five

Kirstin never anticipated the disaster. She'd tackled two rooms upstairs, and that was enough for today. The weather outside was deteriorating fast. A gloomy, eerie wind whistled through the cracks and outside, the waves were thundering on the rocks. Mellie had unexpectedly dropped off in a nap, but it was time to gather her up and take her home before the roads were sticky and slick with ice.

Kirstin only stopped in the bathroom for a minute. All she meant to do was wash her hands. Her gaze whisked around the room. Like every other room in the house, this one had its own special character. The john had an old-fashioned chain pull; the pedestal sink had separate white porcelain taps for hot and cold, and like European bathrooms, it had a bidet. Like the rest of the house, the room was badly dated. The porcelain had cracks; drafts leaked around the windows and some of the diamond pattern tiles were scarred and broken. But those things were fixable. Kirstin hoped whoever eventually took on the project didn't destroy the room's essential character. The bathtub alone was a treasure. The ancient freestanding tub had claw feet and was almost big enough to swim in.

Toweling her hands, she stepped closer to the tub. The shower head was centered, just above, with a brass ring that enclosed the whole tub with a curtain when the shower was being used. Peering at the unusual shower head, she thought the style must be turn of the century.

That was when—out of nowhere, she hadn't touched a thing!—the shower suddenly turned on. Water gushed on her head and shoulders in a cold, drenching downpour.

Momentarily blinded, she shrieked in shock. Jerking forward, she fumbled to turn off the faucets. In seconds the water was off and the deluge stopped, but the damage was already done. Her sweatshirt was soaked, her hair wetter than a drowned poodle's. Shivering hard, she groped for the hand towel.

"For the love of Mike. What'd you do *now?*"

She whipped around at the sound of Zach's voice, her hair spattering water in every direction. "I don't know! I swear the water just turned itself on. I wasn't anywhere near the faucets. It doesn't make any sense. I—"

"Good grief." In that first instant, he hadn't realized how wet she was. "Wait. Don't move. Try not to touch anything else for a whole five seconds, would you? Just... *wait.*"

The only cloth in sight was the miniscule hand towel. He only disappeared long enough to fetch a man-size towel from the linen closet. He flopped it on her head like a mop and started rubbing. She thought she heard him muttering swear words and dire masculine epitaphs about *women* but couldn't be sure.

"I didn't turn on the water," she insisted.

"I believe you."

"I really didn't."

"Kirstin, I believe you."

"I'll bring a wrench up and take a look at those faucets before I go. I can usually fix basic plumbing problems, although I had to admit I've never run across anything like this—"

He lifted the towel off her head and took a look. "Lord. You're a mess. Did anyone ever tell you that you're a walking disaster, Ms. Grams?"

"Ummm..." Self-consciously she raised a hand to her hair. Mess, she suspected, was a massive understatement. Her soaked sweatshirt was drooling water and clinging to her figure in blotches. Even plastered with conditioners, her fresh permanent looked like a corkscrew festival. Wet and wild, it was worse, and what little makeup she wore hadn't survived the deluge.

From the tone of Zach's voice, she'd assumed he was irritated. Heaven knew, she'd given him more than one reason to be annoyed with her today. Yet hidden in the depth of his unruly beard was a definite crooked grin. And when his gaze dawdled down the length of her, he couldn't quite hold back a chuckle.

She'd lost her heart when she saw his infinite patience and gentleness with Mellie, but the sound of that rusty chuckle was an extra punch—a private punch, right between the rib cage. He didn't seem to know he could laugh. The sound of his own chuckle seemed to startle him. In a gesture she was coming to know, he suddenly scalped a hand through his hair.

"What," he murmured, "am I going to do with you?"

"Well, after you throw me off the rocks in the ocean—which I won't mind, I'm really tired of embarrassing myself to death today—I would really appreciate it if you could loan me a sweatshirt. Anything would do. Just something dry."

"I'll find something. Come on, before you catch your death of cold. Change in my room."

She quickly shook her head. "I'd better stay. I don't want to track water all over the hall. Really, if you'd just bring me something, I could change right here—"

"No."

"No?"

Zach took a quick glance around and then sighed. "Humor me, would you? Just for the fun of it, pretend like there's a ghost. A dirty-minded voyeur of a ghost. Anytime you're in this house, keep your clothes on—all your clothes on—unless you're in my bedroom."

"A ghost?" Her lips tipped in a grin.

"Pretty silly, hmm? Come on. Your teeth are chattering."

It was true. She was freezing. Yet she forgot the cold as she trailed him down the hall, stealing glances at his face. She was charmed by his joke about the ghost, and a little touched. Heading for his bedroom didn't bother her—Mellie was on the same floor. Even if a child hadn't been around, Kirstin had no fears he was going to make a pass—not when a few kisses had been enough to shake him. But there weren't many men who were so endearingly shy that they had to invent wholesale jokes to coax a woman into a room alone with them.

Once he'd ushered her inside, he looked back once in the hall and then swiftly closed the door.

"Checking for ghosts?" she asked humorously.

"Have you ever heard of a 'mane'? It's the Roman word for the kind of ghost who wandered the earth, interfering in men's lives. Plutarch believed in manes. So did Homer and Livy—peel off that wet sweatshirt, Kirstin. I'm not looking." He turned away from her and started rapidly opening drawers in the tall chiffonier. He plucked out an oversize black sweatshirt, and tossed it on his shoulder with his back still turned to her.

"I take it you've been reading up on ghosts lately?"

"I found some old books in the house. It was something to pass the time."

"So tell me more." The sweatshirt clung when she tried to tug it off. Her bra was just as soaked, so she peeled it off, too. Her eyes were on Zach, but he never moved his head. He wouldn't, she thought. He was an honest-to-true gentleman. Even if he wanted a woman alone, he'd never take advantage of her.

"Well, there are two kinds of manes. 'Lares' are the spirits of people who've led virtuous lives. 'Lemures,' though, they were the wicked types. Probably criminals. And they get stuck back on earth, unable to rest, until they've righted some kind of wrong. Probably to make up for whatever crimes they committed in their own time."

"Ah." She wasn't really listening. Not that ghost lore wasn't fun to talk about—she loved that kind of stuff—but she was too conscious of being naked from the waist up. Maybe he was aware of her seminudity, too, because he abruptly tensed when she pulled the black sweatshirt from his shoulder. She shoveled the fabric over her head. The thick fleece swallowed her in its warmth and weight, and she should have stopped shivering then.

Instead, she felt shivery in a different way. The scent of him seemed to cling to the fabric. The fleece draped her breasts, feeling as intimate as a man's touch, as *his* touch. The look of his bed was conducive to more wayward thoughts. At least he was sleeping up here now, instead of on that ancient spring-sprung horse-hair couch downstairs. But the rumpled sheets and quilts made it all too easy to imagine him naked in that bed, reaching for a lover in the cold, dark hours of the night. Reaching . . . for her.

Cut it out, Kirstin. If there was ever a man who seemed painfully alone, it was Zach, but that hardly meant she was an answer for him—at least as a lover. She'd attracted Alan, but Kirstin was well aware that most men were more inclined to make jokes than passes with her. Freckles and an ordinary face just didn't add up to femme fatale allure. When men looked at her, they never thought of sex. They thought of friends, and her offer to be a friend to Zach had been sincere. She knew how to be friends. She wasn't at all sure that he could or would ever think of her as a lover, and even the idea sent strange, unfamiliar nerves rattling down her pulse.

"Kirstin? Are you done?"

"Oh. Yes, sorry. Go ahead and turn around." She fingered a quick hand through her hair. When he turned on his heel, his eyes met hers. There was no crackle of lightning. Icy sleet sluiced down the panes of the French doors in a typical Maine winter snow squall. It was pure foolishness, her imagining that crackle of lightning.

"I think two of you would fit in that sweatshirt," he said dryly.

"At least it's big and warm. Thanks for the loan." He was nervous, she recognized. He hustled for the door as if he was in an incredible hurry, now that she was clothed, to get it open before she could worry that he had any tricky intentions. She wasn't worried.

"Where's Mellie?" He seemed to suddenly realize that the child wasn't with her.

"She fell asleep. Curled up in a giant old chair in the third bedroom off the hall. And I really should get her and head home, but while she's still napping, I could take a quick look at your plumbing. There has to be some logical reason that water turned on, and I'm *quite* sure it wasn't one of your Roman ghosts," she said with a chuckle.

"I'll look at it. You don't have to. I've already stuck you with too much to do in this house, and it's late now—"

She knew it was late. And as soon as he opened the door, she surged forward, planning to pass by him, no thought in her mind of doing anything else. It was ac-

cidental, that her hand brushed his sleeve. Accidental, that his eyes suddenly bolted to hers again.

She never meant to kiss him. It was obvious that
she'd made him uncomfortable when she'd kissed him
the first time. Zach really didn't seem to know what to
do with even the most basic gesture of affection. But
she saw the scars of sadness in his eyes again—for a
short time, he'd been so full of fun and humor—and
she thought it wouldn't kill him to discover someone
cared.

She lifted up and brushed a kiss on his cheek.
Nothing more. She never anticipated anything more,
and was already half turned away when he suddenly...reacted. One moment he was clutching her
shoulders. In the next spin of an instant, he wrapped
his arms around her and ducked his head. His mouth
found hers, claimed hers, with aching pressure. It was
like before. He didn't kiss her as if he wanted to, but
as if he had to. As if her lonely wolf had suddenly
slipped the leash on his control.

Her heart thudded wildly in her chest. He filled her
mouth with his tongue, his taste. She told herself she
was afraid, but that wasn't really true. He tasted damp
and warm and male. He tasted like longing and loneliness had been buried, deeply, and for far too long.
He kissed her as if he were a man who was lost, with a
dragon on his tail, and that dragon was going to get
him if he dared let go.

Instinctively, gently, she roped her arms around his
waist and her mouth softened under his. He didn't
have to be rough. She wasn't about to let the dragon
get him. She thought to soothe him, to express understanding. Maybe she didn't know Zach, maybe she

didn't understand anything about his world, but she knew about loneliness. Everyone, sometimes, craved the warmth and solace of another human being.

Her soothing touch seemed to work. Sort of. When his mouth lifted from hers, he laced a chain of kisses down the length of her jaw and throat. His touch was no longer rough. His speed was no longer urgent. It was just... he didn't stop.

His rough beard tickled her soft skin, igniting firecrackers of sensation through her body. He touched her throat with the warm, wet tip of his tongue, igniting more of those sparklers. He leaned back against the wall, drawing her into the cradle of his thighs, his hands pushing at the hem of the oversize sweatshirt until he connected with bare skin. He murmured something against her throat, something low and hoarse, and then aimed for an openmouthed kiss.

The slow, lazy sweep of his lips made her dizzy, deep on the inside. She associated kisses with warm fuzzy feelings. She'd loved kissing Alan. She'd loved Alan. But she never remembered feeling this dark rush of excitement, this restless sensation of spinning wildness.

He half turned her in his arms. His mouth was raining silken damp kisses on her lips when his hand slid up her ribs to cup her breast. Her skin flushed hot and cold. His thumb gently stroked the tip, making it harden and swell, making it hurt, a deep, sweet reckless hurt that she could feel in the depth of her belly. The ache spread, until her whole body felt liquid and heavy.

She touched him wherever she could reach, her hands blindly stroking, exploring, learning him. Their lips found each other in the dark. He cupped her hips, rubbing her against him, making her pulse ricochet and her heart shudder. His arousal pressed against her abdomen, warm, hard, thuddingly intimate.

Fear whispered through her. The first time they'd kissed, her response had been shamelessly uncontrolled. But she'd thought it was just her. Not him. This time she could feel the force and volatility of his desire, and the chance to call a halt was fast disappearing. She wasn't sure if she was ready to be naked with a man. There'd been no one since Alan. There'd never been any man in her life like Zach. There were a thousand reasons, all good, all sound, why she needed to be careful.

Those fears registered in her mind. They were all real. They simply had no power compared to her feelings for him. Her deepest, most feminine instincts, had never steered her wrong. This was right. Her heart believed it. His kiss, his touch, the emotions soaring and spiraling between them, made a song fill her ears. Music. She heard it in her heart; she felt it in the compelling sensation that he was the beat and she was the harmony, and they were tuned to each other as if nothing and no one else had ever existed. She *knew* him. Somehow, someway, he was the lover of her heart. The piece of the puzzle she'd been missing forever and finally found.

"Mommie?"

Mellie's voice called from the distance of the far bedroom. Zach's head jerked up. So did hers. They were still standing against the darkened wall of his bedroom. It took her a second to realize where they were, not just what room, but what house, what town, what planet. Blood was still shooting down her veins with the lick-and-lap heat of a race. And, yes, she heard Mellie, and even logically realized that she should have expected the interruption. But she couldn't seem to feel caught in the act of doing anything wrong. In his arms, she felt so right.

"Moms—?"

"I'll be there in a second, lovebug. I'm right here, upstairs in Zach's room. Everything's fine. You just fell asleep for a few minutes."

Her voice was automatically soothing, reassuring. It reached her daughter, but it didn't seem to reach Zach. She was aware of his jerking down her sweatshirt. Aware of his breath, coming out in rough patches, aware that every muscle in his body had stiffened to stone. But it was his face she couldn't look away from. His eyes glittered in the shadows, dark and dazed, as guilty as if he'd just been caught in the most forbidden of crimes.

"Kirstin...I never meant anything like that to happen."

It hurt, his total and abrupt withdrawal, as if a thousand pins were suddenly sticking into the balloon of her heart. She felt mortified and foolish, for imagining love songs where none existed. She tried to give Zach a tough, strong smile, but it came out wobbly. "It's all right.. I was afraid...I had a feeling, even the first time this happened ... that you probably didn't realize it was me."

"Pardon?"

The light that had been shimmering in his eyes...she had to be impossibly arrogant to really believe it had been for her. She was just...Kirstin. Freckle-faced and flat-chested and ordinary. Alan had loved her, but she'd never kidded herself that she was the kind of woman to arouse fierce, wild passions in a man. "You were lonely. I understood, Zach. I figured that…well, you were probably thinking I was someone else."

Her comment seemed to confound him. "I don't know where you ever picked up such an idea, but the only woman on my mind was you." Zach scowled down at her. "Kirstin…I took advantage of you. And I don't have an excuse in hell."

"You didn't take advantage of me," she denied.

"You don't know. You don't know *me*. I'm an unemployed musician, going nowhere. You don't know what I've done, where I've been—"

His voice broke off when he saw Mellie in the doorway, her sleepy curls tousled and her arms wrapped around her favorite Moose. "Hi, Moms. How come you guys are standing in the dark?"

When Mellie ambled closer, Kirstin instinctively cuddled her daughter with a helpless glance at Zach. There were times he reminded her of the deserted lighthouse on the beach. When he looked at Amelia Anne, sometimes even when he looked at her, the light of emotion in his eyes was bright enough to burn up the night. But he shut that beacon off himself. So quickly, his gaze turned bleak, dark, empty.

"Mom—?"

"I know, honey, it's late and we're going home." She simply couldn't talk to him now. Mellie was squirming and impatient and probably hungry, and they both needed to be home. "I'll be back," she said lamely.

He nodded, and stepped away from both of them. "Kirstin—you don't have to worry that anything like that will ever happen again. It won't. I swear."

That wasn't what she was worried about. She was worried about *him*, unsure what he was feeling but positive it was a mistake to leave him alone. Only what else could she do?

As soon as the front door closed, Zach let out a harsh, pent-up sigh. He glanced out the window. Her truck started with a wheezing cough, but it did start. The skies were pouring sleety rain and the temperature was dropping fast, but it was still relatively safe driving. If the roads had been ice sheets, he knew damn well he'd have made her stay. God knew how he'd have coped then.

He aimed for his jacket in the downstairs hall. A gusty draft of cool air confronted him just as he was jamming his arms through the jacket sleeves.

"Well, now, lad—"

God. Not now. "Are you responsible for turning that shower on her? Are you?"

Jock didn't seem inclined to immediately answer. He feigned the ghostly clearing of his throat. "It did seem a mite good idea for ye to have the chance to see her without a few clothes. You've been moving awfully slow, lad, and I thought a nudge wouldn't hurt ye. She didna seem to mind a bit. The lass had a good sense of humor about that teensy drenching, and I couldna help but notice that the whole plan worked rather well—"

"Hell." Zach slammed out the door without another word. Instantly the sleet bit into his cheeks, and the raw air stung his lungs. He needed gloves and a hat, and had neither. Nor did he care.

He strode for the dark boulders on the beach. The rocks were shiny and slick, the salty wind invasively cold. His body promptly chilled, exactly what he wanted. Remembering Kirstin's warm body wrapped around him, her dulcet soft eyes, her willing, yearning kisses . . . his jaw muscles hinged tight.

He could have taken her. Almost had. He'd wanted her as he couldn't remember wanting another woman. It was more than sex. Her klutzy ways and her dangerously generous kisses and the vulnerable way she showed her feelings . . . he didn't want her being that way with another guy. The way she made him laugh, the way she made him feel good . . . he wanted it just for him. For those few blurred, crazy moments, he'd really believed that the whole damn world would be different, if he just had her.

Selfishness had always been the flaw in his character. What he wanted, he'd always taken. Only he'd never meant to be that way with Kirstin.

His boots slipped on the ice-stained rocks, but he kept going, forcing himself through the slog of memories connected to Sylvie. The two women were as different as sunshine and shadow, but the past inexorably reminded him of exactly why he needed to steer clear of Kirstin.

Sylvie had tracked him down at a concert in Phoenix to tell him that she was pregnant with his baby. Up front, she told him she had no interest in a wedding ring. She only wanted money. A hundred thousand dollars, she'd asked for. Nothing to him, she'd assumed. She seemed to assume a baby would mean nothing to him, either, because she made big promises about his never having to either see or worry about it. It was *her* baby, as she saw it, but she wanted the financial means to raise it right.

Zach had been shaken up, by her, by the whole scene. She had to be nuts to think he would just write her a check. He had no reason to be positive the baby was his—except for her word, the word of a rock-star groupie, a woman he barely knew, and a woman coming across as a lot more mercenary than maternal. Flat out, he told her that he had legal rights affecting any kid of his, and he was doing nothing until he'd seen a lawyer.

That was the last civil word they'd had. She'd freaked out and started yelling, claiming that an unwed father had no rights and never would, threatening that he'd made a mistake in arguing with her because she'd guarantee he'd never see his kid—and then she'd split. It was after she left that he realized she'd shoved a piece of paper into his hand. The crumpled paper was a test report from a medical lab on the blood type of the fetus. It was a rare blood type. The same as his. Maybe in a court that wasn't conclusive proof that he was the baby's father, but Sylvie had risked all the eggs in her basket by bringing it and showing him. That made no sense unless the baby was his.

He'd searched for her. Long and hard. He knew her home was Michigan and hired lawyers to track her down. No dice. It was as if she'd disappeared off the map. Either she'd never given him her real name or she'd changed it; at that time, he had no way of knowing. But finding her without a solid frame of reference such as a name or social security number was a joke. Leads surfaced, but nothing panned out.

In the long months that followed, Zach had ample time to discover what he felt about having a child of his blood, his genes, his heart. He wasn't proud of his life-style, was ashamed of the mess he'd made with Sylvie. But becoming a father was a powerful momentum to change. Finding his child became everything to him.

Almost two years passed—a critical time factor— before a lawyer came up with a worthwhile lead. By the time Sylvie was located, the baby had long been born. A girl. His daughter. But Sylvie had made good on her threat about his never seeing his kid. She hadn't kept the baby, as she first said, but given it up for adoption. A closed adoption.

And Zach abruptly came up against an impenetrable brick wall. In a closed adoption, the identity of the adopting parents was protected behind a mountain of legal rights. Further, in that state, an adoption was permanent and final after a year, meaning that an unwed father could only appeal for rights during that time span. Zach could understand the basis for all those laws. They were meant to protect both the kid and the adopting parents. And they did. It just happened that they left an unwed father like him in a limbo worse than hell.

Zach had one last chance, and only one. If he could prove Sylvie guilty of fraud for failing to tell the adoption agency who the father was, the court might be convinced to reopen the books. And he got her together in a room full of lawyers.

Only she lied. She claimed to have been with a dozen men, and swore that she had no possible way to know who the father was.

It was all done after that. DNA tests could have proven his paternity, but he needed his daughter for that, and no one was going to open the case on the flimsy basis of just his word against hers. It was over. The last legal door was closed, latched and sealed. He could bay at the moon forever, but nothing was going to give him his daughter.

His eyes burned in the sting of wind. The tricks Sylvie had played on him still rankled, but he'd never kidded himself—the sole responsibility for losing his daughter rested on his shoulders. The whole thing could have happened with any other number of women before Sylvie. He'd never been involved with the kind of female that a guy brought home to meet his mother—which pretty much said it all about his judgment and his values and the man he'd become.

Cold waves spattered at Zach's feet. The snow was starting to come down wet and thick now. He should head back for shelter, yet all he could think about was Kirstin.

She saw something good in him. Heaven knew what. Kirstin was so generous and warm and idealistic that she'd probably find something to love in a hardened criminal, so her opinion shouldn't matter. But it did. When he was with her, he wanted to be that good guy she believed in, the guy that put that soul-soft glow in her eyes. The kind of guy who would bite a bullet before hurting her.

It didn't matter if he wanted her. Didn't matter if he needed her. It mattered even less that like a damn fool, he was falling in love with her.

How could he kid himself? He had nothing to offer her but an uncertain future and a past riddled with selfish mistakes. He knew plenty about sex, but his experience with love—real love and commitment—would fit in a thimble. No guy could be less qualified to audition for a role in her life than him.

An innocent had paid the price for his selfishness before. It wasn't going to happen again. The right thing to do, the unselfish thing, was to keep his hands off her. So far she'd made that a little tricky to accomplish, but the future was going to be different.

He wasn't going to touch Kirstin again.

And that was a promise.

Six

"Mom? Do you think he'll come with us?"

"I don't know, sweet pea. All we can do is ask."

"But I get to be the one to ask him, right?"

"Only you," Kirstin agreed cheerfully. As soon as she braked in the driveway, Mellie bounded out of the truck and skipped up the walk. Her mitten-wrapped fists pounded hard and enthusiastically on Zach's front door.

Kirstin felt a twinge of guilt for sending a child to do a woman's work. But not too big a twinge. Every time Zach was around Mellie, his eyes softened and his voice gentled and he suckered right in for her daughter's beguiling ways. He couldn't resist Mellie. She suspected he'd have no such problem resisting a woman who threw blueberry pies at him, tripped over her own feet and embarassingly tortured the poor darling with her unwanted kisses.

After last night, he probably thought she made a habit of climbing all over men in strange bedrooms. Her feminine ego felt as fragile as a critter on the endangered species list. For a few brief moments, she'd actually kidded herself that a potent dose of sexual chemistry had been something else. She didn't need a kick in the teeth to get the message. Maybe Zach needed someone, but that someone sure as petunias wasn't her.

Kirstin didn't intend to put him through any more torture. She'd firmly resolved to keep her hands to herself—but that didn't mean that she was going to leave him alone.

As Mellie continued to pound on the door, lights popped on all through the house, starting on the second floor, then the first, until finally the porch light snapped on and pooled a warm circle of yellow around her daughter.

When the front door swung open, Zach appeared, wearing a baggy black sweatshirt and jeans, his tousled hair gleaming like blue-black sable under the yellow light. She'd known this wasn't going to be easy, yet Kirstin abruptly swallowed. Zach looked as friendly as a club-carrying caveman. His muscular shoulders filled the doorway and she could see his exasperated scowl from fifty yards away. His gaze scanned the shadows. Heaven knew what he'd have done to a Fuller Brush salesman who dared intrude on his privacy.

He didn't discover that the size of his intruder was considerably smaller until Mellie impatiently tugged on his sweatshirt. When he glanced down, that nasty scowl thankfully disappeared—at least while he talked with her daughter. Kirstin watched him hunch down to Mellie's height, listen, exchange a few quiet words of conversation and then jerk his head in the direction of her truck.

That intimidating scowl returned full force as he straightened and strode straight toward her. With her toes squirming in her boots, Kirstin plastered on her bravest smile. She rolled down the window just in time for him to clamp both elbows on the rim. He hadn't grabbed a jacket. He clearly didn't intend to talk long.

"I know I've got this wrong, but I just couldn't seem to understand your daughter. She seemed to be inviting me to a cookout." Zach waited for her to correct this outlandish statement.

"You didn't misunderstand. We're both inviting you on a cookout. You haven't eaten tonight, have you?" It was a rhetorical question. One look and she'd have bet the farm he hadn't given the first thought to food. This close, she felt an inevitable bolt of sexual awareness, and the memory of a dozen shameless, abandoned kisses seeped into her mind. She didn't care. She could surely make those feelings disappear. His face was carved with stress lines and his eyes were shadowed with exhaustion.

Conceivably his tiredness explained why her simple question about dinner threw him for six. His brows shot up, and for a moment all she got was a confused stare. "Ah . . . Kirstin?"

"Yes?"

"Honey, you surely must have noticed that it isn't exactly barbecue weather. It's going to be pitch-black in another hour. It's colder than a well digger's ankles. And it snowed last night.''

Her pulse picked up fresh courage from that "honey." He probably hadn't meant the endearment—it just slipped out—but it was certainly better than his calling her a lunatic. Naturally she knew what the weather conditions were. Four inches of fresh snow covered the roadsides. The pines were laden with it, their long lacy branches sugarcoated with white. "You've never cooked out in the winter? It's the best time."

"You're kidding, of course."

"It'll be wonderful in the woods," she said smoothly. "You don't need to bring anything but a jacket. We've already got food and blankets and kindling in the back of the truck. Mellie and I are old pros at this. And we'd have you back in a couple of hours, max. We won't be driving that far."

"Thanks for the offer, but—" He didn't mean that thanks. She could see from his eyes that he meant a swift, repressive no.

"Mellie?" Kirstin said swiftly. Her daughter thankfully piped right in.

"Zach, there are bears in the woods. Lions and tigers and bears. There won't be anyone to save us if you don't come."

Zach looked down at Mellie. Abruptly he rubbed the back of his neck as if suddenly suffering from a pulled muscle. Whether he knew it or not, his tone turned as soft as melted molasses. "Look, sweetheart, it was really nice of you to ask me. I appreciate it. I really do, but I'm afraid there are a whole bunch of things I have to do this evening—"

"Please, Zach? Please? You can hold Moose. You can have all the marshmallows. You can have the best seat by the fire. It won't be the same if you don't come. And I'll be ascared of the bears."

"For cripes sake, Kirstin, would you help me out here?"

In his dreams. "If you don't come, I'll be afraid of the bears, too," she said mournfully.

"No."

"All you need is a jacket. And gloves."

"No," he repeated firmly, glaring at her, and determinedly ignoring her daughter's soulful, pleading eyes.

"We'll have a great time," she assured him.

Even when he was eventually railroaded into climbing into the truck, he didn't want to go. Even an hour later, when the chicken was neatly speared on a makeshift spit and the blaze of an orange fire lit up the snowy night, Kirstin could see he still wasn't sure how the sam hill he'd been conned into this. She could have told him how. Zach was incapable of hurting a child's feelings. But that didn't mean it wasn't an uphill job getting him to have fun.

Ruthlessly, mercilessly, she put him to work. Someone had to drag over logs for seats, brush melted butter on the chicken, turn the foil-wrapped potatoes on the coals, pour cocoa from the thermos. Zach was the natural stuckee.

Mellie, of course, spilled her cocoa. Just as predictably, she had to go to the bathroom—the instant Mellie was wadded into a snowsuit, she always had to go to the bathroom. Kirstin pawned those dilemmas on Zach, too.

If he'd cooked out before, she suspected it was on a propane-run fancy barbecue. Never over an open fire. Never in the dark, on a night as black as magic, under a moonlit sky that made the snow glisten like white frosting. There was nothing quieter than a fresh snowfall. Occasional flakes drifted down, bigger than quarters and softer than silence. The woods were deep and still, the air redolent with pine. Zach may never have intended to relax, but inch by slow inch, Kirstin watched it happen.

The look of him snagged her heartstrings. Of course Mellie could make a hardened sourpuss smile, and she conspired to keep him busy. But whatever the combination of causes, she'd never seen him ... easy before. Easy with himself, easy with life. The tension disappeared from his shoulders; his smiles started coming free, and though she certainly wasn't going to be the one to tell him, he actually started talking.

"This is going to taste so good, you won't believe it."

"That poor bird's fallen in the fire twice and is charred on one side, and you're telling me it's gonna be edible?"

"You'll see," she teased the skeptic. All three of them burned their fingers. Nobody cared. Their backs froze and their fronts toasted. Nobody cared about that, either. Chicken baked in the oven didn't taste this good. Nothing on earth tasted as good as a hard-won wedge of meat, pulled from the bone with sticky fingers and popped into the mouth when it was still hot and succulently tender. His eyes widened for the first bite.

"Hey, I told you." Scrunched close to the fire, the three of them jostled elbows and ate like starving wolves, which wasn't new for her and Mellie. Zach, though, devoured enough for three men as if he'd just discovered hunger.

"It tastes better 'cause we don't have to use silverware or manners," Mellie explained. "You can make a mess. It's okay. Even if you get it all over you, Mom won't say anything. She isn't even going to say anything if I get the marshmallows now, are you, Mom?"

"Why am I feeling suckered?" Kirstin murmured to Zach, but he just grinned. "Okay, poppet, you can get the marshmallows. They're still in the back of the truck. But first you've got the more important job of finding just the right sticks to roast them with."

"No sweat," Mellie assured her. "I am a *great* stick picker."

Once Mellie pranced off, Kirstin shook her head. "That little monkey has had me wrapped around her little finger from the day she was born. It's not like I didn't read all the parenting books on discipline, but nothing seemed to take."

"You think there's a slim chance she's the light of your life?"

Kirstin chuckled. "Well, sure. But that goes without saying. There's nothing on earth more precious than kids."

"I know," he said quietly.

The sudden grave look on his face caught her attention, but she didn't know what it was about or where it was coming from. "Do you want more cocoa?" When Zach nodded, she unscrewed the thermos and poured the last two cups, then casually mentioned, "I've been meaning to tell you . . . I talked to both your brothers this week."

"Seth? Michael?" Zach was leaned back against a log, his booted foot cocked against a tree limb. His tone registered surprise. "Why'd they call you?"

"Well, I'm not sure, but I've got a pretty good guess." She handed him the steaming mug, careful not to touch him. "You're in Maine. They don't know anyone else in this area but me. I'm not a total stranger—I mean, I've talked with both of them before about the house, several times—and they know I'm in contact with you. They weren't asking prying questions, Zach. They just seem to want to hear from someone else that you're doing okay."

"There was no reason for them to bug you. Hell, I've talked to them a half-dozen times. They both know I'm fine."

"Do they?" she murmured.

He hesitated. "They've both been on my case. They want to know why the band broke up, why I quit."

It was an opening. More than she'd hoped for, but she was afraid of saying the wrong thing for fear of closing it. "I heard one of your tapes," she announced. "A live concert, on some college campus. Wild Nights, I think it was called."

"You gonna give me a critic's review?" he asked dryly.

She chuckled. "Not in this lifetime. People cringe when I sing 'Happy Birthday.' My opinion of anything musical would never be worth any more than hot air . . . but for what it's worth, I thought it was terrific. Especially the last part."

"The last part?"

"The end. The last songs you did at the end of the concert." Kirstin leaned back, using a log as a backrest, with her mug of cocoa resting on a knee. She'd settled a long foot away from him—she didn't want Zach afraid she was going to pounce on him again— but Lord, she wanted to. The idea of wrapping her arms around him was dangerously tempting.

She'd bought the tape of his music on impulse that morning. Until she listened to it, she'd never planned on kidnapping him to the woods with her and Mellie tonight. She'd planned on leaving him alone. Heaven knew her ego didn't need another licking; she wasn't shopping for hurt and heartache; and she was increasingly afraid that any further involvement with Zach would cause her both.

But that tape had replayed in her mind all day. She didn't recognize any of the first songs—but the live audience sure had. In the background, they foottapped and finger-snapped and chanted the words. It was music your body had to move to. None of the lyrics were dirty, but the beat was wild, fast and blatantly sexy. The applause swelled to a scream at the end of each song, and Kirstin tried to mentally picture Zach, his mane of black hair, his hips gyrating in tight jeans, belting lyrics into a mike under hot lights.

It wouldn't work. She couldn't reconcile that image with that Zach she knew. The whole thing struck her as off kilter, strange, impossible. The man beside her had to be bribed and bullied into exposing anything about himself; he was shy and reserved and intensely private.

But then, on the last two songs at the end of the concert, he'd picked up his sax. And Lord, there was his heart, laid open like a naked rose to the rain. Over the sounds of the bass guitar and drums, she heard a longing so deep it made her heart ache. The sax crooned and wailed about a man's isolation and loneliness, a man seeking someone to listen, someone to hear him.

Kirstin knew about that kind of pain. After Alan died, she'd had to be strong, for Mellie, for his family. So she had been, but she'd also known long nights of desperate isolation, times when sadness and grief had overwhelmed her, when she doubted she would ever move past it. No one had been there for her. Not that her family hadn't expressed love, but the hurt had been so deep that she hadn't known how to reach out.

"Hey, where'd you go?" Zach murmured.

She lifted her head. "Sorry. Actually I was thinking about your music. When I was listening to those last songs, I had the strangest feeling ... as if I knew you. As if the music was talking just to me. Pretty nuts, hmm?"

His eyes flashed in the darkness. "No. Not nuts," he said quietly. "That's what good blues is supposed to be about. Communicating to someone else. A way of saying things that you can't say with words."

She watched him swallow the last sip of cocoa. His mouth was so soft, hidden in the rough ticklish beard. He hid his soft side incredibly well, but she'd seen it sneak out when he was with Mellie ... or when a woman touched him with care and tenderness. "You love your music," she said softly.

"Loved, not love. Past tense. It's over for me."

"And that's why you quit? Because you don't love it anymore?"

He set down the cup with a shrug. "It stopped coming to me. It's as simple as that. Blues is about...honesty. You can hit the right chords, play the right notes, but you've got to bring up something from the deep to play good blues. Maybe, like a two-bit politician, I just ran out of lies to tell."

His head jerked up. He clearly never meant to share those feelings. There was a wary look of surprise in his eyes, as if he just now realized how easily and naturally he'd been talking to her.

"I think you could ace a course in being hard on yourself, Connor," she said gently. "People go through dry spells, no matter what kind of work they do. It happens. It's nothing to blame yourself for."

"Yeah, well, you don't know, bright eyes. Maybe I have a lot to blame myself for. You have no idea what rough roads I've been down."

"True. But I have a long history of being an outstanding judge of character," she informed him loftily.

"You think so?" In spite of himself, he started to grin.

"I know so. I'm a good picker of friends. Male, female, young, old—it makes no difference. I can spot a good guy at twenty paces blindfolded. My judgment is darn near infallible."

"Well, hell. Are you trying to tell me that it's a waste of time to tell you all about my criminal past?"

"A total waste. I'm sorry, very sorry, but I'm afraid you're stuck with a friend." Something in his eyes told her that she'd reached him. And something else in his eyes warned her that she'd pushed and pried all he would allow this night. Which was just as well, Kirstin thought, when she glanced up. "Good grief. You poor thing. I'm afraid you're stuck with a second friend, too."

Mellie appeared in the clearing beyond the fire. Her hands were grimy, her face smudged, her stocking cap askew and her arms were loaded down with enough branches to roast a bushel basket full of marshmallows. She launched herself at Zach. "I'm *ready*, Zach!"

Kirstin considered saving him from her overexuberant daughter. Instead, she tucked a lazy arm behind her head and watched. She'd gotten him talking and she'd won a few smiles and she'd gotten him to relax—but she hadn't heard him laugh yet. Mellie flopped down on his lap and coached him in the fine art of marshmallow burning. In trying to help Zach—and talk about wild bears at the same time—she illustrated her conversation with a lot of stick waving. Kirstin gently chided her once, but neither one of them were paying her any attention. It was Zach's own fault that one marshmallow ended up on his face, but holy kamoly. The sticky white gooey square smacked straight in his beard. And stuck there.

Zach tried to pull it off. And did. At least some of it. He looked so shocked. His mouth dropped, and then his eyes crinkled, and then it came. A low tenor of a chuckle, throaty and hoarse, that built into a bigger laugh that came straight from his belly. He roared.

The sound of his laughter made her feel soft, deep on the inside. Lord, she almost hadn't come. She'd almost been too scared. Zach had made it clear that he didn't want her, and to risk another rejection had been daunting and upsetting. It was one thing to trust her heart, and another to rush headlong toward disaster. He didn't seem to feel the fierce chemistry that she did. The building emotional pull, the hunger to be near him, seemed to be all, mortifyingly, on her side.

His laughter reassured her, though, that she hadn't been wrong to reach out to Zach. He'd confessed the problem with his music. She wasn't convinced that a career crisis alone was enough to put the depth of sorrow and pain in his eyes, but from her own life, she knew that the strength to cope with a blow started with the basics. Time, rest, food, fresh air... and hopefully a friend. Someone to talk to, someone to laugh with. And that's all she'd be, Kirstin told herself firmly. A friend.

If she was very, very careful, he'd never know she was falling in love with him.

There was something dangerous about that woman. Zach would feel better if he could just pin down and identify what it was. She looked so innocent; she looked so sweet—but he was no longer fooled. Kirstin could tempt a monk and drive a sane man to drink. Worse, she had the confusing, befuddling, persistent habit of making a man do things that he specifically did *not* want to do.

"You really want it all off?"

Zach glanced up. It had taken two long days to work up the guts to come here. The look of the barber was hardly reassuring. The guy's name was Jim Crow. He stood about six foot five, claimed to be a full-blooded Native American, and had an unkempt mane of hair that boded ominously for his skill with a scissors. Zach had already experienced his sick sense of humor. As quickly as the guy fastened the sheet around his neck, he'd said his calling to be a barber had been a natural. It was his only legal chance to scalp a white man.

"Yeah, I want it all off." Zach fingered his beard one last time. It had taken an hour in the shower to get the last of the marshmallow goo out of it, and damned if he hadn't been laughing the whole time. Laughing. Him. What had that woman done to him?

"Hair, beard, all of it," Zach repeated.

He closed his eyes for the first snip of the scissors. A mistake. Behind his closed lids, waiting for him like a sniper, was the unshakable image of Kirstin's face on the drive home. It had been dark in the truck. Mellie had fallen asleep on the seat between them. Kirstin handled the truck on the icy roads as if she was in a dodge-'em car, and out of the stone blue she'd suddenly asked him, "Do you think I should move out?"

"Pardon?"

"We've been living with my dad for two years now, I think I told you. It seemed like the best idea after Alan died, and it's worked out fine. We're settled here now. Mellie loves it. My dad loves it. But lately... I don't know. I feel so restless. I'm just too old to be living with a parent, and I miss my independence. Does that sound selfish?"

He'd said, "No," briefly, hoping to cut short the whole nature of a personal conversation. They'd gotten far too close during that crazy dinner in the woods. Kirstin was too perceptive, too sensitive. Hell, she could get a man talking before he realized what he was saying. It was just wiser to steer clear of personal subjects. But as if she'd never heard that "no," Kirstin had flashed him a warm smile and just kept on.

"It's just hard, you know? I'm keeping my mom's house, not my own. My dad spoils Mellie more than I'm comfortable with. And it's not like I want to dance around the house naked . . . it's just knowing I can't, with my dad there. Living at home makes everything different. And sometimes I'm so busy being a mom and a daughter that I feel like I'm losing the chance to be just...me. A woman. I mean, suppose I wanted to have a wild fling with a stranger—"

Alarmed, Zach had quickly cut in. "Since when were you considering having a fling with some guy?"

"Since a while. I'm twenty-nine, not ninety. Mellie's asleep by eight o'clock. The nights get pretty long." She'd flashed him another smile. A fellow conspirator's I'm-sure-you-understand-because-we're-both-adults-and-friends smile.

"I don't think you should be considering some wild fling with some guy," Zach had repeated firmly.

"No? Actually I think it's a fairly practical choice. Mellie's my whole life. Any serious relationship I had would and should involve her. But no woman knows how a relationship's going to turn out when it starts. Raising Mellie's hopes about getting another dad—I wouldn't want to risk that. But she'd never know if I had a little fling. And there have to be guys out there who are lonely, too, maybe not ready for something serious, but still nice—"

The kid had fallen asleep right in the nest of his shoulder. Damned seat belts made it impossible to budge her. "Men are not *nice*, Kirstin. No guy is *nice* who's prowling around for a one-night stand. They're all jerks. Every single one.''

She didn't seem to hear him. It was right at the point where she was turning in his driveway. "The thing is, I don't want to hurt him."

"Honey, I've had the feeling before that you spend too much time worrying about hurting other people, and not enough thinking about protecting yoursel..." He'd hesitated. "Hurt *who?*"

"My dad. Or Mellie. They both like the situation as it is. And I don't want to uproot Mellie again when everything in her life is going great. She took it so hard when her dad died. She still misses him sometimes, but at least she's back to normal." Kirstin sighed as she shoved the gear into Park. "I guess it's pretty selfish to even think about moving out right now. Just because I'm chafing at the lack of independence doesn't make it right." She grinned suddenly. "It helped, talking with you, Zach. Thanks."

She'd left him standing in the dark, feeling completely unnerved by the whole conversation. No woman, ever, had read him so wrong. It was almost humorous that she valued what he thought, when the only experience he had was in making colossal-size mistakes. Worse, she'd put these pictures in his mind. Pictures with photographic clarity, of her dancing around a house naked, of her fantasizing about sex with some stranger...

"All done. What do you think?"

Jim Crow whisked off the sheet and spun the chair so he could see his reflection. Zach stared at the mirror in shock. Truthfully the encounter with marsh-

mallows hadn't motivated his decision for this sojourn
with a barber. It was her. He didn't want Kirstin
ashamed to be associated with a guy who looked like
such a derelict. But my God, he hadn't seen his real
face since before his years in the music world. He
felt ... naked. He'd forgotten he had a chin, forgotten that he was stuck with Mr. Clean-cut all-American
looks. He looked ten years younger without the hair.
He'd lost all his toughness.

"I don't suppose you could paste a little of that hair
back on," he said dryly.

"Why, sure. Anything to oblige a customer. I've got
some instant glue around here somewhere—"

Everyone in Maine had a sense of humor, Zach
thought darkly. Plucking the gold stud from his ear—
the earring looked damn silly with a Wall Street haircut—he gave the guy a tip and walked outside, his
mind still on Kirstin.

He could handle his obsession with her skinny legs
and freckles. Hell, that was just desire. Her respect
was what got to him. She'd never made a fuss over his
being a so-called rock star, didn't seem to care if he
had money. She just seemed to like talking to him,
being with him, including him in whatever she was
doing. As if he were the kind of man she valued and
trusted.

Kirstin had him all wrong. He had none of the
qualifications to apply for a relationship with her.
Somehow the sneaky, tricky woman was making him
feel *involved* in her life, but Zach reminded himself
that it took two to tango. Sharing some conversations
was a mile distance from sexual or emotional involve-

ment. Nothing could happen if he didn't cooperate. She was safe. He was safe. Everybody was safe.

Feeling reassured and relieved, Zach promptly folded into the front seat of his Lotus. He had twenty-four nice, long hours before he had to tangle with her again. More than enough time to get his mind off tangling—or tangoing—with even the most dangerous of redheads. Everything, he told himself, would be fine.

Fifteen minutes later he pulled in his driveway.

There, parked right in his customary spot, was her rust bag of an orange truck with the flower decals.

God, he thought, what *now?*

Seven

"It's Thursday, isn't it? Not Tuesday or Friday? I didn't think either one of you were supposed to be here today."

"Hi, Zach! Surprised we're here, huh?" Mellie's cherubic face lit up in a grin. Her cherry-red sweatshirt matched her cheeks and her eyes were dancing. "I told Mom you'd be tickled. We can't stay long, though. Just a coupla hours. Moms has stuff she has to do after this...oh, my gosh. Where's all your hair?"

Zach ignored that question. He slowly peeled off his jacket with a dazed glance at his kitchen. "Holy smokes, where's your mother? And aren't you supposed to be in school?"

"Yup. Only I had a tummy ache. Mom had to come and get me. That's how come her schedule got all turned around for the day. Mrs. Merkel says first-graders have a lot of tummy aches. It's the stress," Mellie informed him. Stress? The look of his kitchen was enough to give a man a heart attack. Cookie sheets and bowls and assorted paraphernalia were heaped on the table. Mellie—and the floor surrounding Mellie—was blotched with the dribble, dribble, dribble of some strange substance. He sniffed. Applesauce? And coating the sauce, and just about everything else, was an equally strange red dust. He sniffed again. Cinnamon. "Sweetheart, what are you *doing?*"

"Making cim'mon art. You know. For Christmas." Mellie carried another spoonful of applesauce from the jar to the bowl, leaving another dribble trail. "You wanna help? It's really fun. First you make cim'mon soup, then you roll it out, then you use the cookie cutters to make shapes. Like angels and stars and reindeers. You know, stuff to put on the Christmas tree. It's easy."

"Where's your mom?" he repeated.

Mellie motioned vaguely to the door. "I think she's working on cleaning some crystal stuff. That's why she gave me this stuff to do, so I wouldn't be in her hair, you know? She's gonna check on me in a coupla minutes, which I told her was silly. It's not like I haven't done this a hundred zillion times before. If you're real careful, I'll let you stir."

Zach didn't want to stir. The only reason he pulled out a chair was some vague notion about exerting some control and order over the mess until Kirstin showed up. Only the kid shoved the sticky bowl into his hands before he could stop her. The next thing he knew, Mellie was spreading minifistfuls of cinnamon flour all over everything. And talking. Hell, the kid could almost—not quite, but definitely almost—out-talk her mother.

"So. What's your theory on the Santa thing, Zach?"

"Theory?"

"I'm not a little kid anymore. We all know that he doesn't come down the chimney. He's just too big a guy. But Julie Brahms—she's my oldest bestest friend back in Albany—she says there isn't any Santa Claus and never was. Only how do the presents get under the tree then, would you answer me that? Don't tell me it's Mom. Mom doesn't have the money to get me all that stuff. And I've seen the reindeer."

"Have you?" Zach shot a desperate glance at the door. He had no idea what "crystal stuff" Kirstin was cleaning, but she never left the kid for long. She'd come any minute and save him. He was sure.

"Yup. I saw 'em in the woods back of Grandpa's house. Not that I'd go around telling people. Tell everybody in school they'd just be jealous, you know. They'd want all the reindeer to live behind *their* houses. But I've seen them myself. Nobody's gonna tell me those reindeer aren't real... you cut them out like *this*, Zach. Haven't you ever used cookie cutters before?"

Zach zipped another harried glance at the door. Dammit, where was she? He'd gotten along okay with Mellie in the woods, but Kirstin had been right there to cover him if he did anything wrong. It was different, being alone with the kid. He didn't know what to do with cookie cutters or messes or how to handle dicey subjects like the authenticity of Santa Claus. This was the kind of thing fathers did.

Awkwardly he rubbed a glop of goo off Mellie's cheek with the edge of a kitchen towel. Hell, it could have gotten in her eyes if he hadn't. When Mellie grinned up at him, his chest hurt.

Everything about those big, bright eyes reminded him of the bridges he'd burned, the rights he'd never have to be a father to his own daughter. His baby was a lot younger than Mellie, but it wasn't that many years before her adopted father could be sitting at a kitchen table, going through a scene just like this. He was the one who was going to be stuck with all those paralyzingly huge choices, such as whether to toot the myth of Santa or tell the truth. Maybe the guy was one of those heavy-dose realists who didn't believe in letting a kid dream and fantasize. Maybe she'd gotten landed with the kind of jerk who was too stuffy to ever get down on the floor and play with her. Dream with her. Have *fun* with her.

Mellie's fingers waggled in front of his nose. "'Case you haven't noticed, Zach, we're done. But I need you to turn on the oven."

"Pardon?"

"You gotta turn on the oven to one-five-oh. No hotter. We're not trying to bake 'em. We're trying to dry 'em. Then they're forever. Only I can't turn on the oven myself because Moms would kill me."

"She wouldn't really kill you."

"Are you kidding? She'd mutilate me. She'd 'mergolate me. She'd feed me to the tigers." This dire future didn't seem to worry Mellie. She grabbed a cookie sheet. "Trust me, it'll be better if *you* turn it on."

"Sweetheart, are you absolutely sure this stuff is supposed to go in the oven?"

"Zach, I'm seven years old," Mellie said impatiently.

Zach gathered this announcement was supposed to give him faith in her maturity and wisdom. He cleared his throat.

"Hustle up," Mellie ordered. "And then, you wanna clean up this mess or should I? One of us better check on Mom. She's on a ladder. It's one of the reasons I've been so quiet. When Mom's on a ladder, you never know what's gonna happen."

Zach's chair screeched across the linoleum. "You didn't tell me your mother was on a ladder."

"Well, of course she is, silly. How else was she gonna reach that crystal stuff by the ceiling?"

The thought finally clicked that Mellie meant "crystal stuff" as in chandeliers. "I'll be right back, honey." Zach jogged for the door. The damn house was loaded with chandelier-type light fixtures. He mentally pictured Kirstin perched on the top of a ladder and nearly broke out in hives. Ms. Klutz would kill herself . . . assuming she already hadn't.

His jog accelerated to a sprint. The chandelier in the dining room was thankfully as dusty as ever, and there wasn't a sign or sound of life in the back parlor. He whipped around the corner of the turret room, and not only stopped dead but quit breathing.

Kirstin was humming, something fast and appallingly off-key, and clearly having a grand old time, totally oblivious to his incipient coronary. The smell of vinegar wafted to his nostrils, the acrid scent apparently coming from the bowl in her hands. The chandelier was an archaic thing, shaped like a pyramid, with dozens of lead crystal prisms dripping from the domed ceiling. She was three-quarters done dipping each prism in the bowl of vinegar, judging from the blinding points of light rainbowing all over the room . . . rainbowing on her.

Stretched as far as she could reach, her arms were nearly buried in the nest of crystals. Every time she moved, the whole chandelier danced and tinkled. She was wearing another skinny ribbed sweater, this one blue, and paired with nothing fancier than old jeans and tennies. But the jeweled rainbows shimmered on the slim tuck of her fanny and the feminine arch of her spine, caught the fire in her hair, trapped the radiance of color on her bare neck.

The old aluminum ladder looked unsteady and he was terrified she would fall . . . that was the only reason his pulse quickened. It wasn't that he associated her with light and fragile rainbows; it wasn't that he felt the most primitive masculine need to protect her; and it certainly wasn't that her sassy behind aroused his hormones with the slam of an avalanche.

It was just that ladder, making him nervous.

He moved forward to steady it. At the same time, she ducked her head and suddenly noticed him. Her jaw dropped in surprise. For an instant, she didn't seem to realize it was him and not a stranger. The bowl of vinegar—God, he should have expected it—skittered out of her hands.

He reached the ladder long before she could have fallen. From the corner of his eye, he saw the splash of vinegar, but the green glass bowl never fell and splintered in a dozen pieces as it should have. It hovered midair, then landed neatly and miraculously right side up on the floor.

Kirstin wasn't paying the bowl any attention. She was too busy twisting around on the ladder to get a clearer look at him. "Good heavens, you scared me, Zach! I almost didn't recognize you!"

He could see that. Her eyes crinkled with humor as she cocked her head this way and that, making no bones of what she thought about his naked face and bare chin and Mr. Respectable haircut. A sister might have looked at him in that teasing, mischievous way.

Only she wasn't his sister. And she suddenly seemed to remember that. The devil of merriment didn't exactly fade from her eyes; it was just that the curve of her lips softened. And she stopped moving altogether. And her gaze glued on his face with an awareness and sexual vulnerability that should have short-circuited all those blazing lights. He could feel the electrical charge in every muscle.

He stepped back, quickly. "I . . . didn't mean to startle you. I was just afraid you were going to fall."

She chuckled again, just as quickly. "You didn't need to worry. I'm real good with heights." She motioned. "Did you see my chandelier?"

Yeah, he saw her chandelier, and he saw all those prisms of crystal and light, and he saw her eyes. And he thought that was the last time, the absolute last time, he was letting her get anywhere near a ladder.

She was gone. They were both gone. The kitchen was shined up, no sign of the applesauce-cinnamon disaster, no sound of the squirt's incessant chatter. Sitting on the floor in the turret room, Zach thumbed open the lid on a beer and took a long swallow. It was peaceful in here, too. The ladder and mess were gone, the blazing chandelier turned off. It was shadowy, dark, quiet.

He didn't miss them. He swallowed another slug of beer and leaned his head back against the rough stucco wall. In his mind's eye, he pictured the last concert he'd given . . . the blinding heat of the lights, the thunder of applause, the sweat and adrenaline power when the music was flowing like blood in his veins. The moment should have been a sustaining highlight of a memory. Most musicians only dreamed of climbing that high, and he'd been there. That's what he should have missed.

Not a curly-headed kid asking him questions he couldn't answer, making noise and messes he didn't know what to do with, climbing on his lap as if she belonged there. And not her mother, either. Zach finished off the first beer, and flipped the lid on a second. She'd done it again. Upset his whole peaceful afternoon, looked at him with those doe eyes, scared him into feeling unnerved and unraveled and . . . restless.

He was thrilled she was gone. Thrilled, relieved and damn near close to ecstatic.

He'd have to be nuts to miss them.

A shadow crossed the doorway as he slugged another gulp of beer. Zach scowled. It was one thing to privately admit a problem with insanity, and quite another to be stuck with incessantly embarrassing proof of that problem.

A sword clanked in its metal holder . . . although, of course, there was no sword. Or anything else in that room but him.

"Whew. Ye smell like vinegar, lad. I couldna help it that some spilled on ye. It was all I could do to save the bowl. Truly it's hard not to notice that she does incline a tad toward clumsiness. Especially around you. I think it's a sign how hot she is to bed ye, lad . . . which is really saying something, considering how you look with all your locks and beard sheared off."

"Go away, Jock."

"Now, now. Ye're sitting here in the dark. Ye might as well have a bit of company. And what are we drinking tonight? Ale? Have ye no good stout rum in the house? Not that liquor can cure what ails ye. She's nicely under your skin, isn't she, son?"

"Nothing," Zach said, "is going to happen."

"Well, it certainly isn't if you keep sending her home."

"I could fire her." Zach chugged another swallow. He wasn't really conversing with a damn-fool ghost, just expressing aloud what had already been on his mind. "I've thought about it, only damned if that isn't the coward's way out. She likes the house and the job works out for her with the kid and it'd hurt her feelings if I fired her. So she thinks she's fond of me. I'll be gone from here in two more weeks. There's no way I'm going to let anything happen."

"She has this way about her. Reminds me of a keg of gunpowder," Jock said fondly. "Ye never know what she's gonna do next. She's good on surprises. I ken just imagine what explosive surprises you'd find between those pretty long limbs of hers—''

"I warned you about talking about her that way. Shut up, Jock."

"Ye're fond of the little lassie, too, aren't ye? Those pretty blue eyes and curly hair... she'll make all the lads dizzy in a few years, I'd gamble, though she seems to have a good head on those little shoulders. Not as impulsive as her mother. I'm thinking the lassie must look like her da."

Zach had thought about Mellie's father all he intended to. The guy had had a straitlaced, stable job in an office. Any time Kirstin mentioned him, he sounded like a considerate saint of a husband and nearly paragon-perfect as a dad. The comparison between Alan and him was enough to make Zach grope for another beer.

"The lassie's such a darlin' that I figure her da must have been a braw bonny man—''

"I don't want to talk about Kirstin's husband."

"Ah. I ken ye." Jock's chortle was a ghostly wheeze. "Ye don't like thinking about her being with another man, eh? But honestly, lad, it's for the best she was wed. Virgins can be a helluva trial. She's no prissy miss, even if she has no been around much. Trust me, she's ripe for ye. There isna a woman born who doesn't need a man—''

"Not in this generation, Jock."

"Pawsh. Things couldna have changed that much. She'd make ye an unforgettable lay, I'm telling ye. It's jest a matter of seducing her. Ye need a bit of instruction, I'm your man, learned everything from Teach, and Blackbeard knew more about women than any man alive, then or now. It'll all work out fine. Her lassie needs a da, ye're clearly mad for her and once you've—"

"Jock?"

"Why, yes, lad?"

"If you refer to her as a *lay* one more time—or even make the slightest reference to her body parts again— I'm going to wring your nonexistent neck."

Silence.

Zach lifted the can to his mouth, and swirled the dark ale around his tongue before swallowing. Two weeks. Two weeks ago he'd come here, asking nothing more from life than a short stretch of peace and quiet. Instead, he'd gotten a woman who was more trouble than a can of worms. A kid who reminded him of the worst mistake he ever made. And a sex-obsessed ghost trying to coach him about love.

If this kept on much longer, he'd be paying rent on a little room with bars. Zach lurched to his feet, thinking wryly that a man didn't have a prayer of being suicidally depressed around here. Who had time? Keeping a lid on his sanity had become a full-time job.

He stood at the window, rolling his shoulders. He didn't need time on a psychiatrist's couch to figure out the ghost thing. Jock was part of his mind. The dark, wicked, immoral part. The selfish part that wanted Kirstin like a claw in his gut. No psychic phenomenon had conjured up that image of gunpowder. It was how he already thought of her. It was how he felt—as explosive and volatile as a lit fuse—every time he accidentally brushed against her. Every time she smiled just for him. Every *damn* time she looked at him with that shy, nakedly vulnerable invitation in her eyes.

A good guy would ignore that invitation. For her—
if it killed him—Zach was going to be that good guy.
He was going to leave her as happy and heart-whole as
he'd found her. All he had to do was last two more
weeks.

And then he'd be gone.

Kirstin had always suspected that this wonderful old
house had hidden treasures somewhere. Still carrying
a flashlight, she bounded down the dusty attic steps,
then the hall and the stairs to the first floor, in search
of Zach.

She found him in the library—unfortunately busy
on the telephone. His feet were crossed on the desk,
the receiver balanced in the crook of his neck and a
mug of coffee was half buried in a mound of strewn
papers. It had to be his brother Michael he was talking to. He always pinched the bridge of his nose and
closed his eyes when he was talking to Michael.

"Yeah, I got it...yeah, I talked to Seth.... God, you
worry more than a mother hen. It's no sweat, I told
you...okay...okay...aw, shoot. Someone's knock-
ing at the door, afraid I have to go."

She had to grin for that outright fib, and then again
for his muttered "Brothers!" when he hung up the
phone. His exasperated tone no longer fooled her.
She'd already seen that Zach kept as close a rein on his
two siblings as they did on him. But his brothers would
worry less, she thought, if they could see him now.
He'd changed so much since he came here. And especially this past week.

She'd been here almost every day, sometimes with
Mellie, sometimes alone. She'd bribed him into tak-

ing walks on the beach, conned him into a dinner in town, sneaked casseroles and cookies into his kitchen. He argued about all of it, but Kirstin had easily discovered that, poor baby, he was incredibly easy to manipulate with guilt. All she had to do was look hurt. He suckered in every time.

If her methods were ruthless, the results were worth it. He'd put on weight. The shadows under his eyes had disappeared. His energy level had zoomed, so much so that Kirstin had the sneaky suspicion that Zach just might be dynamite in action when he really felt good. Fresh air had put the zing of natural color in his face, and she still couldn't get over the change in his looks from the haircut. He'd make any woman look twice with that square chin and strong-boned profile and thick, ruffled welt of dark hair... and she wasn't *any* woman, but someone who cared, someone who knew exactly how lost and angry and exhausted he'd looked when he first arrived here.

Someone who seemed to have fallen deeply and hopelessly in love with him.

Not that he'd ever know. Kirstin slugged her hands into her jeans pockets. "Are you neck deep in something?" She cocked her head toward the strewn papers on his desk.

"Nothing besides being hounded by two nosy brothers. And handling a plague of legal stuff that I've been putting off for a blue moon...." He'd noticed her in the doorway when he hung up the phone, but he hadn't really looked. "Lord, where have you *been?*"

At the direction of his gaze, she reached up. She knew about the dusty smudges on her hands and knees, but not about the sticky spiderweb tangled in her hair. Not that she cared. "I found the attic," she announced.

"Looks more like the attic found you," he said dryly.

"The point is whether you knew there were trunks up there?"

"Trunks? No."

"About ten of them. All locked. I can see you're busy," she said judiciously, "and I certainly wouldn't want to pry into anything that might be private to your family—"

"And horses fly. I've seen that look in your eyes before. Curiosity is killing you."

"Yeah." She grinned. "Would you mind if I took a look? The locks are really old. I'm pretty sure I could jimmy them loose with a little help from a crowbar—"

His boots dropped to the floor faster than stones. Papers fluttered when he swung around the side of the desk. "Crowbar? Just hold up there. I'll come with you."

"You don't have to. You don't have to worry about the locks, Zach, I'll be careful—"

"It's not the *locks* I'm worried about. It's your hide. No offense, bright eyes, but the idea of you in an attic alone with a crowbar is enough to make a strong man shudder. Come on. If we're really stuck doing this, let's get it over with." But it was just wasn't the kind of thing that could be done quickly. An hour later—or maybe two, Kirstin had completely lost track of time—they were still neck deep in dusty debris. The attic windows were too small to provide much light; she'd brought up flashlights and candles to help them

see. Zach had taken a crowbar to all ten trunk locks.
Lacy shawls of cobwebs draped the corners and wind
whistled through the cracks in the plank floor, but so
far Kirstin was the only one impressed with the treasures they'd unearthed.

"What the sam hill is *this?*"

She glanced up. "Haven't you ever seen a merry
widow before?"

Zach squinted again at the candlelit scrap of underwear. "Merry? Widow? Well, I could see how the
guy would be a widow, because his wife would probably die from suffocation if she had to wear a torture
device like this. And what's this?"

"I believed it's called a corselette."

"It looks like chicken-coop wire. I give. For what
conceivable purpose would a woman wear a 'corselette'?"

"It was tied around her waist. The curved wires
were worn in back, to make a woman's hips look bigger."

"That's insane. How'd she ever sit down? How'd
she ever move? How'd she ever breathe if she had to
wear all this stuff?"

"Connor, haven't you got a romantic bone in your
whole body? This is classic Victorian underwear.
You're supposed to notice the lace, the satin rose-
buds, the French seams." But she chuckled when Zach
looked at her blankly.

He hadn't come up here intending to have fun...but
Kirstin could see that he was. Half the trunks were
packed with clothes and momentos from another era.
The women's stuff had bored Zach—until he'd found
the underwear. And another two trunks were jammed

with seaman's lore, ragged parchment charts and light prisms, an eyescope and old-fashioned rain gear.

"Have you thought about what you want to do with all this?" she asked him.

"I'll give my brothers a vote, but I know what they'll say. Toss it. Except for a very few things, we're talking trash."

"Hmm." Her fingertips traced the frayed lace of a Victorian picture frame. The frame was cracked, the lace torn. She wanted to argue with him about saving it, but like everything else, it only had sentimental value to the unknown persons who'd once owned it. "Don't you think it's funny, how everything was just... left? Not just the trunks up here, but the furniture and silverware and linens all around the house. As if someone went on vacation, expecting to come back at any time. It was your grandfather's property, right?"

Zach's head was buried in the seaman's trunk. "So the will said. How long he owned the house is anyone's guess. As far as we knew, he'd never been near the East Coast. His home was in Boulder. Made money in silver years ago. He used to take off for a month every fall to go hunting alone in the mountains. If he was fibbing to the family and coming to Maine instead, we sure didn't know it. We didn't even know he had this place."

"A mystery then," Kirstin murmured.

"I guess."

"You're not curious?"

Zach shrugged distractedly. "There's a lot of women's things here. It wouldn't surprise me if he was philandering around. He was divorced four times. A

helluva bad record, even in his era. None of the Connor men has ever been lucky with women. Seems to be
a character flaw passed down in the masculine gene.
We either pick the wrong women or can't seem to hold
the ones who really matter to us.''

He suddenly lifted his head. His gaze lanced on her
face, then sprang away. He'd wanted her to take his
comment as a joke, Kirstin realized, but she saw no
humor in his eyes. She saw depth and emotion and
something that made her heart clench tight...but that
look in his eyes only lasted for an instant. The view
from a window caught his attention. With a sudden
frown, he jerked to his feet. ''Holy smokes, would you
look at the weather?''

She scooted to his side to peer out the dusty round
window. Lord, when she'd left home, the weather had
been fine. Now a blister of clouds clustered over the
Atlantic, blacker than tarnished pewter, and the snow
coming down was blinding thick.

''Mellie's safe at home with your dad, isn't she?''

''Yes.''

''You'd better get out of here quick. Hell. I don't
like the sound of that wind, and I'll bet the roads are
already a mess. Hustle, honey. Just leave all this
stuff.''

She did hustle, but not fast enough to please Zach.
He flanked her exit down the stairs, found her jacket,
gathered up her tool caddy and purse. Kirstin didn't
doubt that he was concerned about the weather, but he
seemed to make a point of not looking at her. She'd
gotten too close, she thought. They'd been having fun
in the attic and he'd let down his guard. Every time
that happened, he shut off faster than a light switch.

"You've got your truck keys?"

"Yes." She understood that he was leaving soon. She understood that he didn't share even an ounce of the feelings she had for him. She understood that wanting anything else with him bordered on crazy; she had Mellie and a life chock-full of responsibilities. She simply had no choice but to be practical and mature and sensible.

And she was. It was just that no other man had ever made her heart thunder the way Zach did. She'd never felt her palms dampen with the terrible nerves of excitement she felt near Zach. And it hurt, how fast he was trying to get rid of her.

He yanked open the back door, took one look outside and muttered another "Hell." He raked a hand through his hair. "I don't know about letting you drive in this."

"It's okay. I'll be fine. It's only a few miles, and I've driven in Maine weather all my life. Not to worry." The minute she stepped off the porch, the wind slapped her face with the fierce, bitter sting of snow. It wasn't the first time she'd seen a blizzard scare up from nowhere—Maine winters were known for their unpredictability—but this one was definitely mean. She could barely see a foot ahead for the wildly blasting snow, and she only had to take a few steps to realize there was solid ice beneath the first white layer.

Zach, however, was still watching her from the open doorway.

"It's okay," she repeated over the wind. "Go back inside. Really, I'll be fine. I'll see you on Tuesday—" Damn. He had to see her slip and lose her footing. She

didn't crash on her behind, but she recovered her balance just in time.

"The hell it's okay." No hat, no coat, no nothing,
he barreled down the porch steps. "You're not driving on that ice. Get back in here, Kirstin, you're not
going anywhere."

Eight

Zach had just hustled her inside the door when the telephone rang. He grabbed the receiver at the same time he parked her purse and gear on the counter. "It's your dad."

Kirstin pulled off her stocking cap and tucked the phone to her ear, watching Zach with nervous eyes. "No, Dad. I'm sorry you were worried. We were working and lost track of time. I just didn't realize how the storm was coming in ... heavens, it's supposed to get that bad? Well, Zach's a little uneasy about my driving, too, but it's not like I'm a hundred miles from home. Even if it's a little slippery—"

Zach plucked the phone from her hand. "Mr. Stone? This is Zach Connor. It isn't a 'little slippery,' it's a skating rink in the driveway, and it has to be worse on the roads. I'll drive her myself if she has to get home, but as long as you have Mellie taken care of, it makes the most sense for me to keep her right here. There's no reason she can't stay until it blows over. Yeah, I couldn't agree more...try and talk some sense into her, would you?''

He handed the phone back. Kirstin talked to her dad, then her daughter, before hanging up with an exasperated sigh. "Between the three of you, I feel...bamboozled.''

He hung her jacket on the hook next to his in the back hall. "I hope you aren't holding your breath waiting for sympathy. The devil always gets his own back. You have a small habit of bamboozling everyone around you into doing what's good for them.''

"Me?''

"Yeah, you.'' Striding back into the kitchen, he glanced at her with a sudden slow, dry grin. "Lord, you look like you've been in an attic all day. Cobwebs in your hair. Dust and dirt all over you.''

She glanced at the dusty smudges on her hands. "Shoot. The last of my glitz and glamour image destroyed.''

He chuckled. "If there's anything in this world I hate, Ms. Grams, it's glitz and glamour.'' He added casually, "I'll rustle up something quick for dinner. I'm starving. You probably are, too. Then you probably want a shower. Use the one off my bedroom, and if you rummage around enough drawers, you'll find some clean sweats and socks.''

"Zach—'' He was moving too fast. She was still emotionally back at the ranch, feeling embarassed and awkward at his being stuck with her.

"You can sleep in my room. There's a fireplace up there, so it should be warm enough no matter how low the temperature drops.''

"I'm not taking your bed," she said firmly, but his hearing seemed adamantly tuned to only one channel.

"I'll sleep downstairs. It's no sweat. I'm old friends with the couch in the parlor. We won't even be on the same floor, so there's no way you need to feel nervous about staying alone with me."

"Zach. I would never feel nervous about that. I trust you."

She thought she heard him mutter, "Dammit, I know." But she probably misheard him; he was making noise, opening the refrigerator and freezer. "What'll it be? Chicken nuggets, frozen pizza, or the most exciting choice of all—" he waggled his brows with feigned anticipation "—leftovers?"

In spite of herself, she had to laugh. "How about whatever takes the least dishes?"

"My thought exactly."

None of it took long. Zach carted a bucket of firewood upstairs while she popped some food into the oven. They ate on paper plates, whooshed the silverware and glasses under soapy water and that took care of both dinner and cleanup. He kept up a running conversation, but Kirstin could sense it was deliberate. Zach was tense.

She'd been so careful not to touch him, not to even look at him sideways, and had hoped—believed—he was long past feeling uneasy around her. Zach seemed so unsure of himself around women. She never wanted him to feel that way around her, and certainly never wanted him awkwardly stuck with an unwanted houseguest. It was clearly up to her to make the situation easier on him. Deliberately she hung up the kitchen towel, then faked a long, lazy stretch and a sleepy yawn. "I know it's early, but I have to admit I'm beat. Think I'll take that shower and then turn in."

"It's been a long day. I understand." He pushed away from the counter, his expression clearly relieved. "Don't forget. Use the bathroom off my room."

"Still having trouble with ghosts in the other bathroom?" she teased.

"Let's just say that I want to be sure that you don't."

"Trust me, I'm not worried about ghosts, but it really *does* bother me to be taking your bedroom—"

"Are you still arguing about that? I like the couch. I wasn't lying. I'll sleep fine. In fact, I'll probably be warmer than you will."

She doubted that. When she closed the door on his bedroom upstairs, the room was warmer than a cocoon. The blizzard wind raged outside, but not here. He'd drawn the red velvet drapes, switched on the fringed bedside lamp and a merry fire sizzled in the small corner fireplace. It was warm enough to do cartwheels naked, and the pedestal bed was certainly big enough to accommodate all kinds of acrobatic exercise. Not necessarily cartwheels, Kirstin thought. She glanced quickly away from the bed and took a breath.

She'd tried, very hard, not to think of Zach that way.

Tugging her sweatshirt over her head, she figured that her chances of actually sleeping in his bed were about 590 to 1—but she could at least suffer insomnia clean. His bathroom was huge, all ice-white tiles and red-rose porcelain. It was also noisy. The radiator clanked, trying to keep up with the steadily dropping temperatures, and the gale-force wind hissed through the window cracks. She stripped down quickly and flicked on the shower faucet.

The hot pulsing spray steamed the whole bathroom. Standing in his shower, using his soap and shampoo, she thought of him, thought of what it would feel like to expose her naked and freckled and most-imperfect body to him, of whether he'd ever taken a shower with a woman before, of what kind of woman it would take for Zach to shed his inhibitions and reserve and just feel free to be himself.

Not her. That was for sure.

Squeaky-clean, she climbed out of the shower, wrapped one sin-red towel around her body and reached for another. She was just rubbing the second towel on her head, drying her hair, when the lights went out.

A power line down with the snowstorm? Or the house's archaic electrical system acting mischievous again? Whatever the cause, the bathroom went pitch-black. Blindly Kirstin groped for the doorknob.

The firelight in the bedroom provided some illumination, but not much. The yellow flames sputtering behind the heavy metal screen cast more shadows than light. Yanking the towel from her head, squinting in the darkness, she aimed for the chest of drawers where Zach said she'd find some sweats to wear. She saw the antique throne chair, just forgot that its big claw feet stuck out. Her right toe bumped into a sharp edge and she stumbled.

Zinging pain shot to her toe. Instinctively trying to balance, her left hand grabbed for the old-fashioned folding dressing screen. It rocked, then teetered. Then crashed. On her.

She was stunned for a second. It happened so quickly. The screen wasn't heavy, just smothering huge and awkward. Before she had the chance to gather her wits, she heard the pounding of boots and the crash-slam of a door being opened.

"Are you okay?"

"Just fine," she sang out.

His flashlight beam danced around the room until, as merciless as a laser beam, it lanced on her white face. "Sure you are. Lord." In two seconds flat he'd righted the creaking screen. Kirstin had been happier buried beneath it. Her right toe was stinging like the devil, her tailbone smarted; her dignity was never going to recover, and her towel had tangled around her waist. She hustled to yank the terry-cloth cover back over her breasts.

"Just stay still, would you. Don't try to move."

"If I hurt your screen—Lord, Zach, it's a valuable antique—I'm going to have a stroke."

"You think I care about some stupid screen? Dammit, would you quit squirming?"

He pushed back the two-ton chair and knelt beside her. Arguing with him was hopeless. He was determined to check for injuries. Her head first. Gently his fingers sieved through her damp curly hair, searching for bumps or any spot that was tender. She could have told him that anywhere he touched was tender. Her fanny quit smarting and she forgot about her toe. His palm snaked up her right leg, then her left, leaving an electric trail of sexual awareness that Kirstin knew was inappropriate. She knew. But it didn't stop the vulnerable flush of heat from flashing through her whole body. She desperately hoped he didn't notice.

"Zach?"

"Yeah?"

"I'm so tired of being a klutz. It's humiliating and embarrassing and mortifying. I know you probably won't believe this, but I was an extremely skilled computer analyst. Competent. Cool. It's just regular life where I seem to run into this problem—"

"You're not a klutz, honey. The lights went off, it's dark, you were in an unfamiliar room. It could have happened to anyone... does this hurt?"

It hurt incredibly, where his big warm palm gently kneaded her shoulder. But the hurt had nothing to do with an injury. He cocked his head, his gaze probing her face for the reason she'd flinched from him. Her throat was suddenly desert dry, yet just like a wound-up clock, she couldn't seem to stop talking.

"No, it doesn't hurt... and thanks for being kind, but don't waste your breath. Other women don't go through life from one bruise to another. Other women have grace. Poise. I'll bet all the women you knew in the music world were sophisticated and graceful and put-together and cool. Not clumsy. Not like me."

"You're *not* clumsy."

"Yeah, I am."

She wasn't sure why he suddenly swore, harshly, under his breath. She wasn't sure how a debate about her clumsiness could conceivably trigger his fuse. She'd been almost positive that he was finally convinced she'd suffered no broken bones and was about to twist away from her. Instead, he leaned closer.

For a split second she saw his eyes, gleaming as reckless and rich as black diamonds in the fire's reflection. His gaze lowered to her mouth, and then with a groan, he took it. If he wanted her to forget about her klutziness, he certainly succeeded. His tongue dove straight for the dark, damp secrets of her mouth in a wet kiss that made her heart flutter like a dizzy butterfly. Kirstin had the crazy sensation that he'd just jumped off a cliff. With her.

She hadn't known that he wanted her. Really hadn't known. Yes, she'd aroused strong feelings in him before, but only after she initiated the contact, and biology was blind in the dark. He needed someone. She'd never, ever, believed that someone was her. Yet he kissed her like a man staking the most intimate claim. He kissed her as if he'd die if she stopped him. He kissed her as if he were hungry, for her, desperately and only for her, and as if nothing was right in the whole damn world but the treasure of her mouth under his.

Her head was trapped in the crook of his elbow, her hands caught in the fist-hold she had on the towel. She couldn't move. But he could. He peppered kisses down her long white throat, laved the hollow of her collarbone, then came back to her lips. His mouth rubbed, tasted, sipped, then glued against hers.

Her lungs were starved for oxygen. So were his, yet it seemed a hundred years before he raised his head. "You're right about one thing." His voice was low, his usually vibrant tenor as hoarse as the rasp of a rusty nail. "You're different than any woman I've ever known. I never even met a woman who was half as dangerous as you. Dammit, stop me, Kirstin. Just say no. That's all you have to do."

She hadn't expected the question. She hadn't expected to have to make the choice, not tonight, not ever, not with Zach. A well of fear and trepidation swelled in her throat. She had no doubts, not about her own feelings, but she was soul-sure that nothing in her life would be the same if they made love. "Yes," she whispered.

"Sweetheart, that's the wrong answer."

"Yes," she said again, bolder this time. The longing in his eyes made the answer come easier. The longing, the loneliness, the primal bond of emotional connection she saw in his eyes . . . her heart was beating to the same rhythm. Never once had her heart steered wrong. It was just that with him, it was impossible not to be scared. She was risking so much.

When she leaned up and fused another kiss between them, though, his volatile response eclipsed any fears she had. Zach was taking risks, too. His fingers shook, when they sieved through her hair. His shoulder muscles were clenched with control, and in the depths of his eyes she saw naked vulnerability. He wasn't used to feeling vulnerable. He clearly didn't know what to do with it.

"I swore I wouldn't touch you. I swore I wasn't going to let this happen. I don't want you regretting this."

"I won't."

"I don't want you hurt."

"I won't be."

"I can't make you promises."

"I'm not asking you for promises."

"I have protection. I wouldn't risk you. Damn. I don't want you worried that I planned or expected this, because I didn't. It's just that I've carried protection around since I was eighteen. I was taught that was something a man automatically did. It's nothing I even think about anymore. That's the only reason I happen to have—"

"Zach," she whispered gently, "you're talking too much. You don't have to be nervous. Not with me."

The word "nervous" seemed to startle him speechless. His mouth, for that breath of a second, gaped open.

Kirstin could have kicked herself for the tactless comment. She'd meant to reassure him, not dent his masculine pride. No man liked to think of himself as nervous or inexperienced, but Zach's unsureness around her had the obvious source. It wasn't as if she thought he'd never been intimately involved with a woman, but heavens, she'd been married. He hadn't. She knew everything about lovemaking, which made it obviously up to her to take a tactful, guiding role.

"Ah...honey? I'm not exactly sure how you formed the idea that I was nervous, but if for some reason you're thinking that I don't know what to do—"

"Shh." She pulled off the towel. That ended the conversation.

His gaze riveted the length of her bare firelit skin. He made a sound in the back of his throat. A rough, keening groan. The next thing she knew, he'd scooped her up. With his mouth laced on hers, lanced on hers, he carried her to the door...which he slammed with a foot...to the dresser, where he fumbled blind in a drawer for protection...and finally, to the bed.

He dropped her. It was an easy fall into the plump feather mattress, and he didn't abandon her long. His sweatshirt was gone when he climbed onto the bed and dove, straight for her. His chest hair was thick, black, wiry, the texture ticklish and erotic against her bare breasts. Her total awareness of him threatened to swamp her senses, but she tried, desperately hard, to keep a clear head. Any minute now, he could need her help. Any minute now, he could get nervous again. The first time with anyone was always more anxiety than pleasure. It was hard to relax. Reality could never possibly measure up to expectations, especially when you wanted something so much, too much. It'd be good—she'd help make sure it was good for him, but she was way too old to really expect the earth to move.

The room, the house, the whole planet spun when he tumbled her beneath him. The fire hissed and the wind blew, but not where they were. She thought she knew so much, and abruptly discovered that she knew nothing at all. Not about making love. And not about him. His palm skidded over ribs, hips, thighs, exploring her, cherishing wherever he touched. He wreathed kisses around her breasts, cupping the soft swollen flesh for the touch of his mouth. His tongue licked and lapped, silky wet, hot.

The look in his eyes could have melted silver. He'd never let go before. Not with her. The fierce liquid sheen in his eyes made her wonder if he'd let go before, ever.

Jewels of sweat beaded on his brow. The corded muscles of his shoulders shone like gold. His skin was hotter than a sauna, his heart beating fast...and then faster yet. He bent his knee between her thighs, rubbing the rough denim against her softness, exulting when she catapulted toward him. His reward for that response was another rain of kisses, carnal, explicit, earthy.

She couldn't catch her breath. He didn't want her to. He palmed the nest between her thighs, nuzzled the tips of her nipples into aching peaks, took her mouth again and again. She told herself it was crazy to associate innocence with him. He knew more about sensuality than she'd ever dreamed of, more about her body and arousing a woman than she'd even known herself.

Yet it was still innocence she sensed in him. There was no practiced skill, no deliberateness. In his eyes was the well of a man's wonder, dark and spinning deep; in his touch was a hunger to give, not take, and a laying bare of tenderness. His face was harsh with concentration and a terrible vulnerability, as if he didn't please her, something terrible would happen. As if the only thing he could hold on to in the dark abyss of the night was her.

She didn't know what to do—she'd never known what to do with Zach—except love him. She matched kiss for kiss. Her hands stroked and caressed, telling him with her touch and her eyes of her desire and need for him. Textures, sounds, scents blurred into one sensation. *He* was her sensation, until the only thing she knew was how he made her feel and how far, how fast, they could both burn up before the fire exploded.

The bed sheets rustled. The blankets bunched. Their hands met at his belt buckle. Both battled to unlatch it. Zach clearly was in no mood for humor, yet he suddenly chuckled in the darkness... and so did she. In that instant of laughter was the richness of intimacy and anticipation.

And then his face turned grave. "Kirstin...I'd lose an arm before hurting you. I can still stop."

"Maybe if the house were on fire, I could, too. But I'm not promising. Where the devil is that dreadful little packet?"

"Sweetheart, you're not helping my self-control."

"Good. I can't think of anything either of us needs less than your self-control. If you want to be helpful, though, you could do something with those jeans. Like toss them out in the snow? I'm pretty sure you're not going to need them for a while. I love you, Zach."

She'd meant to keep it light; she sensed that Zach was afraid of what was happening between them, but those nasty, impulsive three words just slipped out. It changed things. He cupped her face in his palms and kissed her again, thoroughly, completely, as if responding to the depth of feeling in her voice in spite of himself. All she knew was that he lost it after that. He left her to cope with his jeans. An awkward task when he wasn't trying to help and seemed to have forgotten all about them.

Kirstin had the brief sensation of contributing to her own demise. He had no problem remembering what to do when those jeans were gone. He liked naked against naked. He liked teasing her. He liked everything that made her body different than his, which he showed her without mercy. Cavemen had taken their women by firelight. The look in his eyes was that old, that basic, that alluring. A woman could drown in emotions that deep. A fragile, vulnerable woman could break, tangling with a tiger, unless that tiger was gentle with her.

Her tiger was unforgettably gentle. It had been so long that she was scared he would hurt her. A foolish fear. She was ready for him; he made sure of it. When he took her, he whispered coaxing, reassuring words, love-song words of longing and belonging. It was music she already knew, music she would forever and uniquely associate with Zach. The rhythm was the same as her own heartbeat, the drumbeat of his pulse inseparable from her own. He was her love, and by the time they hit soaring speed, she'd already taken wing.

It wasn't her fault—there was no way she could have stopped herself—from whispering again, "I love you, Zach."

Zach couldn't sleep. Hell, maybe he'd never sleep again. He stopped pacing around the dark bedroom long enough to push aside the drapes. The storm had finally abated. Snow was mounded in every corner and crevice in windswept peaks and mountainous drifts, but the night had turned innocently clear. A dreamer's full moon nestled in the blanket of a black satin sky. A lover's moon, he thought, and turned around to look at Kirstin.

She'd stolen *his* side of the bed and *his* pillow, and she was sleeping deeper than an exhausted puppy. Zach rubbed the back of his neck. She *should* be sleeping, after what she'd done to him.

He still wasn't sure what happened. She'd started talking about being clumsy, about *feeling* clumsy, and something had cracked inside him like an earthquake fissure. Kirstin was not only beautiful, but she was the best woman he'd ever known. It seemed terribly important that he tell her that, only he was lousy with words, so somehow he'd ended up kissing her instead. It made sense to him at the time. Still did. Another man—any other man—would have understood that kind of logical reasoning.

He just never anticipated her taking him under. She'd *made* him lose control. Where Kirstin got the confounded idea that he was an innocent in bed was beyond Zach, and then she'd said she loved him. She upset him. She'd been upsetting and confusing him

from the day he met her. That damn redhead persisted in making him feel things he'd never felt. She
made him feel whole. She made him feel like a man
who was worthy of being loved, and the way she came
apart in his arms... hell. He'd have happily sold his
soul for her and never looked back. No human male
alive could have resisted her, so he had a justifiable
excuse for losing control... the first time.

Zach rubbed the back of his neck again. Technically the second time had really been her fault, too.
Totally her fault. They'd been all sweaty and sleepy
and she'd been lying next to him, wearing that incredibly silly smile and nothing else. And then she'd tickled him.

Making love was supposed to be a serious business.
Making love was the measure of a man's performance, a test of his adequacy and prowess and skill.
It wasn't about *tickling*. When she discovered the spot
between his third ribs was vulnerable, she'd burrowed
under the covers and attacked him. He had to pin her
down. There was no other way to get her to stop. He
had to. And he was stuck kissing her after that because she was asking for it. The tilt of her lips and her
dancing eyes and the wicked drumroll thing she did
with her hips... she was asking for trouble, all right,
she was begging for it, and she just made it impossibly hard...

To be that good guy he'd promised himself to be.

You swore you wouldn't hurt her, Connor.

You swore you wouldn't be selfish. Not with her.

Impatiently he grabbed his flashlight and strode
barefoot for the door. He couldn't just...stand there.
Every time he closed his eyes, he started hearing music in his head. The notes, the chords, the song he as

sociated with her. One of these days he was going to have to write it down, just to prove to himself once and for all that it wasn't real.

But not now. He was too restless and edgy to even think about that now. Soundlessly he turned the doorknob and let himself out.

He'd barely released the door when he realized he had company.

"Well, I surely don't need to ask if it went good. Ye look destroyed, lad. Nice long marks on your back, and I do believe she sank her teeth in your shoulder, son. Did I na tell ye it would be special with her?"

"Shut up, Jock."

"Ye dinna want to share the details?"

"No."

"We're both men, after all. This is an area where I could easily offer ye some pointers. And where ye headed in such a fire of a hurry?"

"The fuse box. The lights went out hours ago. Possibly the blizzard knocked out a power line, but with the outdated electrical system in the house, I figured there was an equal chance that . . ." Zach whipped his head around. "*You* didn't go anywhere near those fuses, did you, Jock?"

As he should have expected, there was no one in the gloomy dark hall to answer that question.

Downstairs in the room off the pantry, freezing his bare feet on the cold linoleum, he found the high amp fuse sitting all by its lonesome on the utility shelf. He replugged it back in, then strode to the foot of the stairs. The power was back on, judging from the wedge of yellow light coming from the hall.

When he started trudging back up, the hound caught up with him.

"Did ye tell her, lad?"

"I don't believe you messed with that fuse. I don't *believe* it. And did I tell her what?"

"Did ye tell her ye love her?"

A lump formed in his throat, as big as a thick clay stone. He almost had. When she'd been lying beneath him, her arms laced around his neck, that butter-soft loving sheen in her eyes...the words had almost sneaked out. And all the terrifying power of emotion that went with those words. "No."

"Don't kid yourself, lad. Ye'll no find another like her, and a true love doesna happen to everyone. Ye'd be a fool to throw it away."

"You know nothing about it."

"Then ye havena told her about the babe yet, either?"

Zach's jaw clenched.

"Aye, I know about yer child. It took me a time to figure it out, but I've heard yer nightmares in the night, yer calling out in your sleep. I dona quite comprehend why it's such a trouble for ye. Ye wouldna be the first man to sire a child from the wrong side of the blankets. But if it's weighing on yer soul, just tell her, lad. She'll understand, I promise ye."

Zach didn't buy property on the San Andreas fault line. He wasn't about to believe promises from a ghost. Yet, upstairs in the hall, he flicked off the light switch, and stood outside his bedroom door in the dark, suddenly unmoving.

He wanted desperately to believe that Kirstin *would* understand...but he didn't see how. She'd said it herself. Nothing was more precious to her than children. And the baby he'd lost was never far from his conscience.

Guilt pulsed through his temples. For reasons he'd never fathomed, Kirstin believed in him. For reasons he could never comprehend, she'd trusted and respected and liked him from the start. He'd been damn near suicidally depressed when he came here. Not now. Zach closed his eyes. Knowing Kirstin had changed him. Maybe his feelings had started with protectiveness—hell, it was a full-time job watching out for her. But it had become more complicated than that. And more simple. Her smiles had become something to earn, her respect something he valued. Maybe the strength to change had simply come from wanting to *be* the man she thought he was.

Kirstin cared about him. Now. But God knew what she'd feel if she knew about his baby.

Zach took a long breath. There was no way, of course, that she'd ever know...unless he told her. Maybe he could never have helped falling in love with her; maybe making love with her had been equally inevitable. But if he was really that good man she believed in, he'd protect her from hurt. To do that, he had to make her believe she hadn't made a mistake by becoming involved with him. When he left, he didn't want her to feel ashamed—of anything they'd done together, but especially of him.

Which meant that he couldn't, ever, risk telling her about the child.

Nine

Kirstin closed the back door with the swing of her hip. "Zach?" *Man,* it was cold out there. She set down her tool caddy and purse with a thunk, then peeled off her hat and ice-crusted mittens. Her heart jackhammered as soon as she heard Zach's boot steps.

"You're late. I was getting worried about you."

"Didn't mean to make you worry. One of the houses I caretake—the Fergusons'—had a window blown out in the snowstorm. What a disaster! There was a huge drift of snow, right in their living room, glass everywhere, one antique table just plain ruined. I had to call them, then their insurance company—some guys came out right away to fix the window, but I couldn't leave until they were done. And then traffic slowed me down. The roads are still a mess from the blizzard, complicated by every Christmas shopper in the county determined to be out today—"

"Okay, what is it? Whenever you talk nonstop, I know there's something wrong."

"Heavens, nothing's wrong."

"Then something's different. And you're not looking at me. What'd you do to yourself? Turn around."

"In a sec. I'm honestly dying for a cup of coffee." Kirstin blew on her cold hands as she strode for the stove. "I've been thinking about what still needs doing around here. The house has finally shaped up, hasn't it? There are just a few more rooms that need tackling—the solarium for one and you still haven't decided what to do with those trunks in the attic—"

"Kirstin."

She felt his big hands land on her shoulders and firmly twist her to face him. One look at his eyes, his face, his mouth, was all it took to start up a symphony of awareness in her pulse. It was disgraceful, how easily he turned her on. At the vast age of twenty-nine, she'd never expected to find a man who turned her knees to noodles and her heart to mush. Nor had she ever found a man who terrified her more. Lord, she was scared.

Making love with him had changed everything for her. The two days they'd been stuck in the blizzard had mostly been spent in his bed. Regrets? She had none. Zach had made her feel beautiful and treasured. He'd made her feel differently about herself as a woman, more of the woman she could be, *wanted* to be. To never have loved him? To never have known him as a lover? She'd trusted her heart, in spite of the emotional risks, and refused to regret it. There was no way she would take back even a single moment of the time they'd had together.

But she'd hoped, really hoped, that she wasn't alone in those feelings. In so many ways Zach had expressed love. But he hadn't said it, and her vulnerable, foolish heart already felt ripped raw at the thought of his leaving. Even the slow sneaky grin stealing over his face couldn't make that rawness disappear.

"I knew there was something different. What's this?" He touched the thin metal frame on her brow.

"Glasses." The lenses were steamed up. She plucked them off to rub them clean with a towel, then perched them back on her nose. "I had an eye exam last week. You know how klutzy I am, Zach. It's not like I thought anything was going to make that problem miraculously disappear, but it was time I had my eyes checked anyway. As it turned out, I was embarrassingly myopic. I mean, don't you think I would have realized it before this? I—"

"Would you quit squirming? I can't even see how they look."

She couldn't quit squirming. Vanity was so stupid; she'd never fallen prey to that silly vice before, but Zach was such an extraordinarily good-looking man. It wasn't as though she had a prayer of adding glamour to her looks, but spectacles were like ... well, like freckles. Not a flaw, exactly, but another nail in the coffin of ordinary, another shout of how much her looks were a contrast to his. "I know they look silly. And doncha think I'd have had the sense to choose something besides red frames with my hair—"

"I like the red frames. And I like the glasses on you. But I thought we'd settled that business about your being klutzy before."

His sudden scowl was extremely intimidating. Ruthlessly he wrapped her arms around his neck. She wasn't exactly sure why he lifted her to the counter. With painstaking care he removed the glasses from her nose and folded them neatly.

"We have work to do," she reminded him.

"It'll wait. This won't." He stepped between her legs. She abruptly discovered why he liked the counter. It put his mouth on a level with hers. His eyes on a level with hers. And she'd seen that wicked, unprincipled caveman gleam in his gaze before.

"In the kitchen?" Her voice came out like a squeak.

"It's one of the few rooms we didn't have the chance to christen during the storm. Not that you can't get out of this if you want to. This is a multiple guess test. If you answer the question correctly, you're off the hook. Is Kirstin Grams a clumsy klutz, or is she the most graceful, sensual woman I've ever met, ever known, ever dreamed of?"

"Zach . . . you don't mean that."

"Wrong answer, honey. And now you're stuck paying the price. Poor baby, are you ever in trouble. Don't even try begging for mercy, because you asked for this. . . ."

She missed part of his dire threats because his voice was muffled when he pulled off her sweatshirt. And right after that she couldn't protest because he was already kissing her, his mouth latched on hers as tightly as a key for its lock. How could she have said anything? She was too busy kissing him back.

His playfulness was hopelessly irresistible, because he'd been so sad. He was reaching out for life again, reaching out with needs and feelings, and he made it so easy. With him, for him, it was just so easy to let go, to just let her senses explode on his taste, his smell, his textures, to let nothing else matter but how she felt and how she could make him feel.

She had love that was dying to be expressed. Holding it back was painful, while giving was so natural and easy and right. It was no longer winter when he touched her. It was a daffodil and hyacinth kind of spring, and she was spring young again, back at the time in her life when anything was possible and love was everything. He loved her with that kind of richness and promise. Zach had to know what they had together.

He simply had to.

The next afternoon, Kirstin wasn't scheduled to work, but she just stopped by for a few minutes with Mellie. Baking snickerdoodles was a seasonal event for them, along with hanging mistletoe and holly and making cinnamon tree decorations. Mellie had insisted they bring Zach a batch of the still-warm cookies. Kirstin set them on the kitchen counter, but Zach wasn't around. Lights were on, a fire blazing in the parlor hearth, but his jacket was gone from the hook.

"Well, we'll just leave them, lovebug. He'll find them."

"But I wanted to see Zach."

Kirstin knew she did. "It can't be helped, sweetie. He's gone somewhere. You'll see him another time." They were stepping down from the back porch, headed back for the truck, when she heard the music. So did Mellie, whose face instantly lit up in anticipation.

They rounded the corner of the house, slogging through snow as tall as their boot tops, when Kirstin suddenly grabbed Mellie's hand.

She spotted Zach, but he didn't see them. Kirstin was fairly positive that he didn't see anyone. The temperature had warmed up, and the ocean was quiet today, a lead-silver bed of water with the sheen of a mirror. Spray dampened the rocks on the shore. The deserted lighthouse was shrouded in smoky mist. He was standing on the rocks, wearing jeans and an unzipped leather jacket, and the gold of his sax gleamed in the late-afternoon light. His eyes were closed.

It took her a moment to identify the song he was playing. The old rock-and-roll tune was before her time, familiar only because one of the radio stations regularly concentrated on old golds. "Take Good Care Of My Baby." That was it. Only Kirstin had never heard it the way Zach was playing it. The notes pouring out of him was a ballad of the heart. She heard all the pain and poignancy of love; she heard a man tearing himself in two; she heard a man expressing the most unbearable kind of hurt.

"Mom, let me go. I wanna give Zach a hug."

"I know you do, lovebug." Lord, there were tears in her eyes. And another batch of them was threatening to spill over.

"I don't wanna go home. I wanna see Zach, and he'll want to see me. I *always* give Zach a hug."

"I know, sweetie." She knew exactly how her daughter felt about Zach, exactly how he was with Mellie. It was part of what made it impossible for her not to love him, impossible not to believe what a special family they would make together. But there was no time to indulge in those kinds of yearnings right now. Mellie's lower lip jutted out. With a sigh, Kirstin scooped her up. It wasn't often she carried her two-ton seven-year-old, but Kirstin had been a mom too long not to recognize when her offspring was about to set in her stubborn heels. "I'm sorry, Mel, but this time is different. We don't want to bother him now. What he's doing is private to him. It wouldn't be right to intrude."

"I think private is *stupid!*"

"I know. It's a hard thing to understand."

"I think that thing you said about 'truding is stupid, too!"

Her priceless angel, Kirstin thought, was scaling up to a full-blown temper tantrum. She managed to keep the volume scaled down until they were both seatbelted in the truck behind closed windows. The jewel of her life had a temper that was one of those experiences of motherhood she wouldn't have minded passing on. Even while soothing Mellie, though, her mind was on that music. On him.

Zach was playing again. Weeks ago, when he'd arrived, he'd looked so exhausted and heart-worn that she'd never been surprised he was having trouble working. No matter how much you loved something, anyone could burn out when the body was stressed out and fatigued. Truthfully she'd thought the burn of pain in his eyes came from somewhere else—from grief or loss—but that was before she understood his fear of never playing again. Music had been his life. The threat of losing something that important to him had to be frightening.

He'd just needed food and rest and exercise. And maybe, she wanted to believe, someone to love and care and believe in him. She'd done that. If he didn't love her, if he never loved her, she felt good about being part of that for him, someone who really *had* helped. And she unquestionably had, hadn't she? If he was playing again?

But the chords of that music were still tearing at her heart. Driving home, trying to placate Mellie, trying to talk, trying to keep her eyes on the snowy roads and slick patches, her throat felt thick and her tongue acid-dry.

She'd gotten him to talk about everything under the sun—growing-up escapades, fathers and brothers, politics and life and things he loved—but Kirstin had always been aware that Zach had a deep, private side. There were corners he didn't want touched, doors he never opened. He wasn't a man who easily expressed his feelings, and Kirstin had always understood that it would take time for him to really trust her.

Only she was fast running out of time. The music she'd heard had compellingly shown her that the man she loved was still bruised on the inside, and the inescapable reality was that she didn't have a prayer what to do for him. If he couldn't tell her what was really wrong—or chose not to open up—there wasn't much she could do. Except ache for him, deep on the inside. And remind herself, even if it hurt like the fresh stab of a knife, that he'd never made promises, never talked of love. Maybe, very simply, because he didn't love her.

And he was leaving.

Very soon.

Well, it was done. Kirstin piled the cleaning supplies into her tool caddy. The jalousie windows in the solarium had been a pistol to wash, and her arms and fingers ached from the project, but it was the last one. Naturally dust and dirt were still going to accumulate, and the house truly needed an electrician and plumber and carpenter to update the whole thing. But every room in the house was at least livable now. She'd done all she could.

The thought depressed her. Wanting a break, and hoping some fresh air would cure the doldrums, she grabbed her jacket and climbed the stairs to the third floor. A small arched door led to the widow's walk that wrapped around the top story. She stepped outside, and breathed in the tangy salt air. A misty haze had settled over the cove, silvery gray, putting a pearl shine on the snowy landscape. The ocean lapped on the rocks, splashing up diamonds and then stealing them back, the rhythm of the sea more ancient than time.

She was listening to the gulls cry, her arms hugged around her chest, when Zach stepped out on the porch behind her.

"I figured I'd find you out here."

She smiled. He pulled her back against him, automatically snuggling her close with a nuzzling kiss near the shell of her ear. Even wearing her jacket, she'd been starting to freeze. That was never a problem when Zach was close. "You can imagine ships out there, can't you? Whalers and schooners and maybe pirate ships with white sails and a black flag...and I can imagine someone's wife up here. Waiting. Pacing the widow's walk, worrying if her man was okay. If she had a spyglass, she could see any ship that came in the harbor."

"You like the thought of pirates, do you?" Zach murmured.

"Only the wicked ones." She grinned. "The ones bringing trunks of emeralds and diamonds and pearls to their lovers . . . in between, of course, pillaging and plundering and running around flashing those pretty silver swords.''

''They were thieves.''

''True. But if you have to be a thief, you might as well be a romantic one.''

He nuzzled her neck again. ''All those pirates probably had scurvy and black teeth.''

''Not in my imagination, they don't.''

''Kirstin.''

''Hmm?''

''Honey, I can't stay much longer.''

Kirstin knew it was coming. She knew. Even so, his quiet voice hit her whole body like a blow. She turned in his arms and looked straight into his eyes. They'd both been avoiding the subject, and one look at his face told her that he was wary and worried about bringing it up now. Maybe that was how she found the strength to come out with a lie, not just a little fib, but possibly the biggest whopper she'd ever told. ''You're afraid I'll be hurt, aren't you? Don't be, Zach. I made my own choices. I knew long before we made love that you could only be here for a short time.''

The edge of his thumb brushed her cheek. ''It's not that I want to leave. I don't have a choice. There was no sweat about my taking off a month to deal with this house for my brothers, but I left a life dangling. My place in L.A.—there isn't anyone taking care of it. Unfortunately somebody had better collect my bills and pay 'em. Like me. And there are some legal loose ends about breaking up the band still pending. They affect other people, not just me. I have to take care of it.''

"I understand." He'd never talked about managers or the other members of his band or any of the ties he had in the music world. Just then, those things didn't concern her. He did. "What about you? Have you done some thinking about what you want to do?" she asked him softly.

"Yes." He hesitated. "I've been working with score sheets for the past couple of weeks now. Writing songs again."

She'd guessed. She'd caught him several times in the turret room, fooling around with the keyboard, a pencil stuck between his teeth, concentrating so intensely that he'd never realized she was there. It wasn't the same music she'd heard him play by the ocean, and it was equally different from the brash, sexy rock on his tapes. These songs were new, fresh, vibrant with emotion. At least one of the pieces he'd been working on was a love song, the chords haunting and poignant. The song had no lyrics, but to her, it communicated...innocence. The innocence of a man discovering the wonder of love for the first time.

Kirstin had warned herself—how many times?— that she was probably dreaming up what she wanted to hear. "So..." She cocked her head. "You're planning to play again?"

"No. Not in public. Not again. Ten years is enough of living in a fishbowl, at least for me. But I know damn well there are kids who feel differently."

"Kids?"

He scalloped a hand through his hair. It ruffled right back in the wind. "You can't imagine how many of them there are, Kirstin. Kids, loaded with talent, willing to sell their souls for a chance on a stage. They just need that first break. But the problems start happening when they get it. The crowds, the drugs, the bright lights, the fast life—they're exposed to it all so fast that half the time, they don't know what hit them. And the kids who are the *real* musicians are more vulnerable to falling into real trouble than the others. Ah, hell. I'm not sure I can explain...."

"I'm listening. Try," she coaxed him.

Zach leaned back against the railing, his words coming out halting and slow. "It's about being a musician. It's not just the life-style that's a danger, but the whole nature of what you *do*. You learn to play what you feel. You learn to express all your emotions through the instrument. And that's great—it's part of the high—but it's dangerous, too, because you're not connecting with *people*. It doesn't seem to matter at the time because the music is everything. You don't know you're lonely. You don't know you're losing sight of what really matters. Can you understand?"

"Yes." She understood that for the first time, he was talking about *him*.

"I don't know if I can save any kid from making the mistakes I did. But what I *do* know is that I have a way to connect with them. Songwriting is always what I did best, what I love best, and that would be my hookup— I'd lease out use of the songs, working with kids trying to make a start, coach them on the music itself..."

He hesitated again, his gaze searching her face, as if he were hoping to hear something from her. Understanding? Support? Heavens. Kirstin could have given him that easier than breathing. "Zach, the whole idea sounds great. You'd be terrific working with kids. I really think you could make a difference in their lives."

"Well, I don't know about 'terrific.'" Self-consciously he rubbed the back of his neck, but he was relieved that she liked the idea. Her support mattered to him. "I've made a few calls," he admitted. "Enough to know that I could put something together. And I think this is something I have to try."

She saw. It was more than a dream he was sharing with her; there was purpose and determination in his eyes. As she'd guessed all along, Zach could be an unstoppably formidable force when he set his sights on a goal. He was more healed than he knew, she thought fleetingly. She wanted to feel joy for him—and did. Only she was painfully aware that his plans excluded her.

"So..." She gave him her most brilliant smile. "When are you planning on leaving?"

"If my brothers have their way—Christmas Eve. Michael sent me a plane ticket. Lord knows how he managed it—at this time of year, he must have either killed someone to get it or seduced someone's sister at the airlines. I didn't want to fly—what the hell would I do with my car? But he had an answer for that, too, contacted someone through the airport who'd drive it for me. Anyway, the flight leaves out of Bangor on Christmas Eve around noon with a connection in Portland. I'd be in Atlanta by dinner. The three of us need to get together to come to a decision about this house. Seth and Michael are both hot to do that over Christmas." He looked at her. "I could stay here through the holiday. I really don't give a damn when I settle the house business with my brothers. I could just throw the ticket away."

"From the way you've described Michael, he'd have a stroke at the cost if you did that. I can understand their wanting to be together with you for the holiday. And you're going to be busy after that. Who knows when you'll have another chance to talk together about the house?'' She heard her own voice, sounding so logical, so sensible. Yet the most illogical, idiotic song popped into her mind. A Christmas song. The one about the child who only wanted one thing for Christmas, his two front teeth. Kirstin didn't need teeth. She didn't need presents. All she wanted from Santa was... him.

She and Mellie could uproot in two seconds—if he wanted them. She could find work anywhere; Mellie would be happy as long as she was in a loving environment, and though her dad would miss them, he would surely understand. You never threw away a chance at love, he'd taught her that, and she'd never cared where she lived. Starting over with Zach would be an adventure, nothing she was afraid of—which he'd find out so easily, if he would just ask.

''Kirstin...'' He stepped toward her.

He wasn't going to ask, she realized. And it wasn't pride that held her back from offering, but the painful knowledge that she'd already thrown herself at him too many times. There was simply no way she could force him to see that they had something strong, something precious, something infinitely worth fighting for. Not if he didn't feel it.

His knuckles tucked under her chin. She looked up, to find his eyes locked on her face, his expression intent, grave, worried. And she responded the only way she could. ''It's okay,'' she said softly. ''It wasn't a fling for me. You're not a fling. I knew I'd miss you and I knew it would hurt, but I also knew ahead that we only had a short time together. You never broke any promises to me."

"I don't want to hurt you. I never wanted to hurt you. If I've done anything to make you regret being involved with me—"

"Don't think that. I don't regret a single moment we've had together."

He almost smiled. "If you ever needed me, I'd be there. So fast it'd make your head spin." His fingertips brushed her cheek, his touch as tender as his eyes were a loving, luminous blue. "You gave me my music back," he whispered.

"No." She shook her head. "You did that yourself, Zach. You just needed some time and some rest—"

"I didn't need time. I didn't need rest. I just needed you. There was never anyone in my life like you, Kirstin. And there isn't a prayer on this earth that I would ever forget you."

Then damn you, Connor, she thought desperately, why are you breaking my heart?

Ten

This wasn't going to be tough, Kirstin promised herself, because she refused to let it be. It was already past nine, which meant that Zach had to leave for the airport in less than an hour. That left no chance of their staying long or any awkward, lengthy partings. All she had to do was smile and say goodbye and wish him the absolute best. How hard could that be?

She pulled into his driveway in her father's Oldsmobile. Her dad had never asked about her feelings for Zach, but Kirstin suspected he knew how deeply her heart was involved. "Be careful," Paul Stone had told her that morning, and given her a monster-size hug.

Kirstin braked and turned the key, thinking that it was far too late for her to be careful. She leaned up to check her appearance in the rearview mirror. It was Christmas Eve, giving her a natural excuse to dress up, but motivating her far more had been sheer feminine pride. Zach had never seen her in anything but jeans before.

Her navy angora sweater with the big cowl neck kindly hid her lack of curves; the short white wool skirt showed off her legs. Boots were a dratted requirement because of the snow, but she'd left her practical Beanes' in the closet and opted for a fancy pair with heels. Heaven knew how she was going to walk in the three-inch suckers, but she truly didn't care. The permanent-from-hell was now a month old and had finally toned down. Loose, rusty brown curls framed her face; a touch of mascara had darkened her pale lashes, and a little gloss and blush added color. A plain Jane couldn't instantly turn into a Lorelei, but she was as beautiful as she was going to get.

Heartbreak, thankfully, didn't show.

"Mom! What are you *doing?* Let's *go!*"

Kirstin swallowed the ominously threatening lump in her throat and came up with her most cheerful smile. "Okay, lovebug. I'm ready. Would you like to carry the present?"

Her red wool coat almost caught in the door, but she saved it in time. That seemed a good sign that she wasn't on klutzy mode today, and truly, the weather was perfect for the holiday. The skies were clear, the sun blazing bright on the snowy landscape and the air was stinging fresh and exhilarating. It was a day to lift anyone's spirits.

Zach must have seen the car drive up, because he opened the door just as Mellie was raising her mittened hand to knock. It was a good thing he had his arms opened, because Mellie flew right into them.

"I don't want you to go, Zach! I love you!"

"Sweetheart, I love you, too."

When she saw his big strong arms around her daughter, that ominous lump loomed in her throat again. She wondered if Zach even knew how instinctively he held Mellie, or how rare and special the emotional bond was between them. Mellie was going to miss him. Badly. But Kirstin suspected he was going to miss her far more.

Not enough to make him stay, though. She saw his duffel bag and instruments parked near the door. He was clearly ready to leave. When he released Mellie, he lurched to his feet with their gaily wrapped present in his hands. All his attention focused on her.

She stepped forward with the last of her courage and pressed a cool kiss on his cheek. "Merry Christmas, Zach."

"What did you do?"

"It's nothing. Just a little present—"

"I didn't mean the present. I meant you." He peeled off her coat, his gaze zipping down the length of her, then back to her face, her mouth, her eyes. Damn him. He looked at her as if she were the most beautiful woman he'd ever seen, as if he were memorizing every inch, every pore, as if he couldn't bear to let her go. And he just stood there. Holding her coat. Looking at her with a fierce, torn expression of longing in his eyes, and—she could have sworn—love. Double damn him, but she was going to cry if he kept this up.

She tried twice before she could get any volume out of her voice. "We won't stay long. We both know you have to be on the road soon. We just wanted to bring you the gift."

"Yeah, Zach. Open it up! Come on!"

He moved then. "Come on in the kitchen. I happen to have a couple of presents for you two, and I don't think everything's so put away that I couldn't make a quick pot of cocoa."

He'd bought Mellie a huge new Moose, not to replace her ragged and bedraggled stuffed animal, but so her "moose would have a pal." For Kirstin, there was a small wrapped package in red-and-silver paper with a lopsided floppy bow. Inside, she found a pendant, a pair of solid gold musical notes dangling from a delicate chain. Zach cleared his throat when she touched it. "I didn't know what you'd like, Kirstin. I don't know much about shopping, but I thought maybe it would make you think of me sometimes... *damn*. Don't *do* that."

"I'm not crying. I just got something in my eye. It's beautiful, Zach, precious. I love it." She bent her head while he attached the clasp behind her neck. His hand lingered on her nape before shifting away from her.

It was his turn then. She'd hand knitted the muffler. It was a shocking bright blue, nothing like the subdued hues he usually wore, but she thought it was the same unforgettable color as his eyes and the wool was as soft as a cuddle. "I was afraid it was too startling a color—"

"It's a perfect color."

"I couldn't think of what to give you. I'm just not very good at thinking up clever presents, and you never seem to have a scarf when you go out. I just wanted to know that you'd be warm—"

"Kirstin, I'll treasure it. I couldn't love anything more."

He draped the soft wool around his neck, and then just looked at her again. No one had touched the cocoa he'd poured. His refrigerator had been emptied, all dishes washed and put away, and now the kitchen was a minidisaster of bows and wrappings and clutter again. The clock was ticking over the sink, yet neither of them moved to put anything away.

Silence stretched between them, as taut as an arrow quivering in a bow. Kirstin dropped her eyes. "I'll bet that your brothers will be anxious to see you. I'm glad you're going to have the chance to get together with them over the holidays."

"Are you having extra family over tomorrow?"

"A houseful. Every stray aunt, uncle and ragtail cousin comes for dinner on Christmas—along with every neighbor who doesn't have family around. It was my mom's theory that no one should be alone on the holiday. My dad used to tease her that she'd ask the whole army if he'd let her. Anyway, having a houseful has become kind of a tradition. It's always chaotic and noisy and a little crazy—"

"It sounds like fun."

Nothing about the whole silly, awkward conversation was fun, Kirstin thought, but it was better than that poignant, aching silence. "You'll let me know what the three of you decide to do about the house?"

"Yes. I'll call you in a few days. We'll put it up for a vote, but I already know my brothers want to sell it. You'll continue to take care of it for us in the meantime?"

"You know I will."

"No climbing in the attic. No cleaning chandeliers. You don't have to do anything but make sure it's still standing."

His teasing voice was nearly her undoing. She lurched to her feet and started scooping up the present wrappings. Only Zach lurched to his feet, too, with the bright blue muffler still hanging around his neck, and instead of sensibly helping her clean up the debris . . . he reached for her.

"Kirstin. . .I can't leave like this." One of his hands sifted gently, softly through her hair. His voice lowered to an achingly halting tenor. "I thought I could. I thought I could leave, as long as I knew you cared about me. But this is impossible."

"I don't understand."

He let out a rough sigh. "There's something that I need to tell you. It's something I never wanted you to know, because I didn't want you to find out anything that would change your feelings about me. This sure as hell will, but it still needs saying. I can't have you thinking that I could just *leave* you. As if I could walk away. As if you meant nothing to me. As if I weren't so in love with you that I can't see straight. . ."

Her heart stopped, then restarted at a thundering pace. He couldn't possibly know that those words of love had dropped the whole bottom out of her world. She started to respond, but Zach interrupted her. "Look. It may take me a minute to say this. Maybe we'd better be sure what Mellie is up to first."

She glanced around swiftly. Mellie had been in the kitchen only seconds before, skipping around the table with her new Moose. Now she was gone. Kirstin's eyes shot to Zach's. She had no idea what he needed to tell her so desperately, but all that mattered was the emotion she saw in his face. His gaze was chock-full of love, full of what she'd dreamed of, what her heart had hoped for, what she'd *believed* he felt at a soul level.

He clearly wasn't going to talk, though, until they had a guaranteed private moment together, and that meant tracking down Amelia Anne. Kirstin whisked toward the doorway. "You know how Mellie loves to explore this house. I'll just make sure where she is and what she's doing."

When she called from the hall, there was no answer. When she called from the bottom of the stairway, there was still no response from Mellie. Worry never crossed Kirstin's mind. Not at first. Mellie loved curling up on the window seats, hiding behind draperies and playing make-believe games. The house was full of alcoves and niches to appeal to a child, and sometimes Mellie concentrated so hard that she simply wasn't listening.

But Kirstin searched the whole downstairs and still couldn't find her. When Zach met up with her, back in the hall, he started calling and searching, too.

"Ye like it, don't ye, lassie? All the gels like jewels and lace."

"It's really for me?" Mellie fingered the long rope of yellow pearls around her neck.

"A' course it's for ye. Now climb on me lap and I'll tell ye a story about pirates—and a princess just like you."

"You're almost as fat as Santa Claus. And I like the way you talk."

"Well, that's good, 'cause we may be here awhile. Ye probably never heard of the Brethren of the Coast, bein' young as ye are. Some said Blackbeard was the most notorious pirate of the time, but t'was never true. T'was me all along. Now picture it—my sloop had six cannons and a full complement of seventy men—"

"You're sure I can keep the necklace? I don't have to ask my mom?"

"I'm sure, lassie. Now pay attention. I was running with Teach's ship at the time, the *Queen Anne's Revenge,* when suddenly a gale wind came up. On the horizon we saw a dozen British ships, warships all, manned to the gills they were...t'was in the middle of a storm like ye never seen, and they were aiming straight for us. A cannon fired. It hit the rigging, then the deck, and lar, there were men running everywhere. One fell in a pool of gory blood. We listed bad ... I'm telling ye it was a mess, lassie. No chance of getting out of it alive, none a'tall, even with all me wits and cunning—"

"Are you going to get to the part about the princess soon?"

"Now, lassie, we dona want to rush through the best part of the tale—"

"The best part is gonna be when you save the princess."

"Though ye may not believe this, me darlin', that's exactly what I'm trying to do. Save your princess of a mother. Now where was I? Ah, back in that bloody mess ..."

"Zach, she would never have gone outside without asking, and her coat's still in the hall. Honestly there's no reason to panic. When she's playing really hard, she just doesn't hear things." Kirstin cast a frantic glance at the wall clock. "Lord, the time. You're going to miss your plane if you don't leave now. I'll find her. You don't have to worry—"

"To hell with the plane. You think I could leave without knowing she's okay?" Zach yanked on his jacket. "This is my fault."

"There's no *fault* involved." Kirstin fetched her wool coat. Going outside was pure foolishness, but Zach wouldn't listen, and she wasn't about to leave him alone. For the past twenty minutes he'd been wired up and upset beyond all reason. "She's probably just hiding out, being mischievous. It wouldn't be the first time. And there's certainly nothing you should feel responsible for."

"I should have been watching her."

"Connor, could you try to calm down? If she was hurt in any way, believe me, we'd know. If Mellie so much as stubbed her toe, we'd be hearing about it at the top of her lungs. And anyway, *I'm* the mom. If anyone should have been watching her, it was me."

"You don't understand. I *know* you're the mom, but she was here, in my house. I should have watched out for her. I *always* watched out for her, and I swore that nothing would happen to any child because of my being careless, ever again."

"Again?"

Zach couldn't answer her, not at that moment. It was too terrifying thinking of a seven-year-old loose, alone, this close to the ocean in the winter. The shore water was shallow but cramp-cold, and the currents could be unpredictably powerful. The rocks were slippery with salt spray. A little body could slip and fall so easily, and the defunct lighthouse had unquestionable allure for a kid, any kid, and it wasn't just *any* kid who was missing. It was Kirstin's Mellie.

It was *his* Mellie.

He couldn't stop for the panic, couldn't talk, couldn't think. The squeezed-tight fist in his chest wouldn't ease...until he jogged the perimeter of the house. He circled twice before he was finally convinced that the only tracks leading to the ocean and the rocks were his own big boot prints. There was enough snow so that he could be absolutely sure. Her little footprints would have distinctively shown up.

"Okay..." Kirstin caught up with him at the back porch, and snagged the sleeve of his jacket to catch his attention. "That's enough. She's in the house, not out here. We'll find her, Zach. You're shaking. There's nothing about this that's scary. She's just *playing* somewhere. I want to know what's wrong, and I want to know right now. What did you mean about being careless about a child *again?*"

Maybe he'd have said it differently if he hadn't been shook up. Maybe he'd have had the brains to couch it, soften it, make himself look not quite so bad, but somehow the whole thing tumbled out. Maybe it was just too late for anything less than total honesty.

"I made a woman pregnant, Kirstin. She had a baby. My baby. I didn't know her. I didn't know anything about her when I got involved. She was angry when I didn't give her money right off, angry with me, angry enough to make sure I never saw my kid. She gave it up for adoption. I never had a say. I never had a choice." His throat felt as if it were full of gravelly stones. "That's what I didn't want you to know. That I was the kind of guy who would be careless about a child. But I was. At the time I was thinking about *me*, no one else, not what kind of woman I was getting involved with, not how easy it is for birth control to fail, not anybody or anything else but me. I lost her. I lost my baby. For no other reason than I was a selfish jerk.''

Kirstin wanted to say something, but for that first instant, the words couldn't seem to get past her throat. She'd always known there was something he was holding back, some problem so deep that it had infected his whole life. But he'd done such a good job of convincing her it was related to his heart's work, his music. She just wasn't expecting this . . . but Zach was clearly expecting her to judge him. He was braced like a reed in the wind, as if he anticipated the hurricane blow of her condemnation. His eyes were bleak, as cold as the burn of blue ice, and she finally knew where that haunted look of pain came from.

When she didn't instantly respond, Zach swallowed hard and then jerked around. She reached for his arm, but he didn't see. He was already bounding up the porch steps. ''Look, it doesn't matter now. We have to find Mellie.''

Her watch claimed it was past ten. Even if he had a pair of wings, Kirstin didn't see how he could make his flight from Bangor now.

She trailed him up the steps, looking at him instead of where she was going. Zach spun around at the door, as if he somehow knew at just that moment she was going to stumble and trip. He grabbed her by the elbow, not thinking about it, just doing it, and once she had her balance he simply moved on and past her, as if nothing more were involved in that quick instant for him. But there was for her.

Protecting a woman was as instinctive as breathing for Zach, she thought. He was a man who would always save her from stumbling, a man who'd saved her from ''ordinary'' and opened up her life to possibilities. What she wanted for herself, for her life, was different because of knowing and loving him. With sudden painful perception, Kirstin realized that she'd given herself credit for taking all the big risks in involving herself with Zach.

She hadn't known, then, that Zach had taken the most monumental of risks in daring to care about her.

She peeled off her coat and damp high-heeled boots and padded in her stocking feet to the hall. Zach was already there...and so was her daughter. Mellie looked as if she'd been playing in a dustheap. A string of yellowed dusty pearls bounced almost to her waist, and a collar of tatted lace was wrapped around her second-best dress. She was skipping down the stairs.

"God, baby, where've you *been?*"

From the fourth step up, she took a flying leap into Zach's arms, talking ten for a dozen at the same time. "I've been having a *blast.* I made a friend, a secret friend, and we've been telling secret stories in a secret room. You push this piece of wood in the blue bedroom and that's all you have to do, *poof,* there's my secret room, and it's full of all kinds of bloody stuff..."

Kirstin blinked. "Amelia Anne! Where did you hear language like that?"

"Language like what? You wanna hear a story about a princess, Zach? A princess with flat boobies who was 'ttacked by pirates?"

Kirstin blinked again. It wasn't the first time Mellie had come up with wild tales or conjured up secret friends, but she couldn't fathom where the language was coming from.

She said nothing, though. Zach had scooped up Mellie as if her seven-year-old weighed less than thistledown. Cocoa seemed to be the only critical priority on their agenda. Her daughter claimed to have a bloody big thirst.

The pot was still warm on the stove. Kirstin did the pouring. Mellie was too busy weaving wild stories about a redheaded princess, and Zach was too busy listening. She hadn't noticed before how alike they were. Mellie was the only one with the cocoa mustache and chubby legs, yet it was oddly uncanny. They both had sky-searing blue eyes, both unruly black hair that tended to wave and tuft in cowlicks. Any stranger would assume they were related. They looked, she thought, like father and daughter.

Finally Zach glanced up—not at her; he'd carefully avoided looking anywhere near her for more than a half hour—but at the clock over the kitchen sink. "It can't be eleven."

"It is. I'm afraid you don't have a prayer of making that plane, and on the holiday, I don't think all the gold in Fort Knox would buy you a seat on another one." Kirstin rinsed out the two empty cocoa mugs. "Zach, I'd like to drive Mellie home. Would you come with me?"

He hesitated. "I'm not sure that's a good idea."

She was. Her small clan didn't do much on Christmas Eve but anticipate. Tomorrow was the unstoppable day of rituals and traditions, present unwrapping, setting the table with her mother's silver, a houseful of company, lemon meringue pie and cookies in tins and bayberry candles scenting the house...Kirstin didn't know if Zach would willingly be part of any of those rituals. She didn't know anything at the moment, except that Mellie could begin the ritual of anticipation with her granddad. And that she needed to be alone with Zach.

Even for a klutz, she had her moments. He had to call his brothers to let them know he hadn't made the flight, he said. She let him. And then she firmly, smoothly, gracefully herded him toward his jacket and out the door. She shepherded him toward her dad's car, not his, because that sleek black Lotus was capable of eating up fast miles in the wrong direction. She had a feeling Zach was close to bolting. He'd had enough of Maine, and after that confession, he'd had enough of talking. Maybe he really believed he'd said all there was to say.

Mellie kept him distracted and busy on the drive. When Kirstin pulled into her dad's place, though, Mellie flew out in a rush to tell Gramps about the princess story and her new secret friend. That left them suddenly alone, and from the look on Zach's face, he suddenly realized it.

Kirstin saw his hand on the door handle, and gracefully reversed in the driveway at burning rubber speeds. He reached for the seat belt instead. "Where are we going?"

"The woods."

"You're not dressed for a walk in the woods. You'll freeze in that light coat."

She didn't care if she froze. She'd have worn a bathing suit in a blizzard if it would have helped erase the stiffness and tension radiating from Zach. And she didn't want to go back to the house. She wanted a place that was unique and special to them. Zach had opened up to her for the first time in the woods. And she'd discovered, there, that no bomb or tornado or avalanche could stop her from falling in love with him.

The clearing where they'd roasted chicken was bright with sunlight melting on snow. Icicles dripped from the pines, glittering like jeweled prisms. No one had discovered their private spot. Even their log seats were just as they'd left them. But she didn't sit and neither did he.

Zach climbed out of the car and slugged his hands into his pockets. "Kirstin...if you brought me here to break it off, you didn't need to. I never had to be a Philadelphia lawyer to figure out how you feel about babies and children and the kind of man who'd risk either one. You don't have to tell me it matters."

"Yes, it does," she agreed quietly, and then hesitated. "When I first met you, I had the strongest impression that you were grieving for someone you'd lost. I thought I was wrong, because your brothers had told me that you'd been physically ill, but I still couldn't shake that strange feeling of empathy. Now it makes sense. I know all about grieving for a loss, Zach. I lost both Alan and my mother. It's not something you can recover from in a week or a month. I don't think you're supposed to. Love wouldn't mean very much—life wouldn't mean very much—if we got over our losses as easily as the blink of an eye."

"Honey, my baby is very much alive. It's not the same thing."

"No? You lost someone who was part of your heart. I'd call that grieving by anyone's definition. And I wish you'd trusted me enough to tell me before. Have I done something to make you believe I wouldn't understand how hard that kind of loss is?"

"No. Yes." He touched a leafy pine branch, making a dozen icicles dance in the sun. He didn't see them. "Dammit, Kirstin, you're confusing me." He scalped a hand through his hair. "It's not that I was afraid you wouldn't understand. It's not the *baby* I didn't want you to know about. It was me. The kind of man I was."

Kirstin nodded. "You were unhappy. In fact, it took me forever to understand how you could possibly be comfortable in a life-style where you had to stand up in front of thousands of people. But that wasn't the hard part, was it? You could put on a mask for a crowd. You made a choice to give them your music, but they didn't touch you. The distance of a stage made sure you didn't have to get too close. It's never easy being vulnerable, risking exposing yourself at a heart level, and that has to be even harder for a painfully shy man."

"Sweetheart, there isn't a soul who knows me who would *ever* call me shy."

"So you're good at fooling people. You expect me to be impressed? You're the shyest man I've ever known, Zachary Connor." *There,* she thought. His shoulders had been so ramrod stiff, his eyes so brilliantly avoiding hers. But she was finally getting through. He stopped walking and turned to face her. The look of yearning in his eyes was so intense, so fierce, that she could barely stand it.

"You were always so determined to think good things, nice things, about me that weren't true. I was never the good guy you thought. It's more than tarnish on a halo. Honey, I never *had* a halo."

"Thank heavens," she murmured. "The last thing I'd want is a saint. When I was a teenager, I wanted a hero—a white knight to rescue me. Thankfully I grew up. I seem to collect an unfair amount of bruises along the way, but I can rescue myself. I don't want a hero and I don't need one. I want a man I can talk to.

Someone who accepts me for myself, who I can change with, grow with, and yeah...share my nights with. Someone recently taught me that I have a lot of shamelessly wanton urges, and I'd like a man who made me feel open and free and honest about exploring those feelings. But I'm not looking for a perfect hero to love. There's no character in a man who's made no mistakes and knows nothing about life. Perfect is an undesirable trait. In fact, it's of no use to me at all."

There was no smile, but a little more of that tension eased out of his shoulders. For a moment. "I didn't just make a small mistake," he said quietly. "I made the kind of mistake that affected a child's life. It's hard for me to believe you could forgive that."

"Forgive? I'm not the one having a problem with forgiveness, Connor." Kirstin shook her head. "I admit I've always seen this from a woman's point of view. It's easy for another woman to take the side of an unwed mother. I never thought about the emotional pain of an unwed dad. Until you." She lifted her face. "I want to tell you the obvious—that you have every reason to believe your baby is happy and thriving. Every adopting couple I know was screened right down to their toenails, and the chances are they were dying for a baby to love and care for. It's not the same as having the right to raise her yourself, but rationally, logically, you have a hundred reasons to believe she's fine. You're the one who isn't. And the problem is what we're going to do with this guilt of yours."

"Kirstin—"

But she wasn't about to let him interrupt. Not just then. "You seem to expect me to judge you. Fine, I will. But I have no way to judge you for something you did back then. I only know you now. I've watched you put yourself through hell, which has told me all I need to know about the kind of man you are." She hesitated. "It was through loss that I discovered the power of love, what really mattered to me, what was really important. You've been going through the same grieving process. I don't think you're the same man you were, Zach. Maybe you didn't respect that guy. Maybe you didn't like him very much. But if you'll take off the blinders, I think you'll see that you're a man infinitely worth loving."

Zach said nothing for a moment. He just looked at her, the same way he'd looked at her when they first met...as if she were plumb crazy, missing half her apples upstairs. She'd thought he was going to reject her then. She thought he was going to reject her now. Maybe, though, just maybe, she'd taught him a little something about listening to his heart.

His smile came slowly. First, no more than a twitch at the corners of his mouth. Then an outright, daring curve of his lips. And finally the smile reached his eyes, with a fierce warm glow that lanced on her face with treasuring love. "Honey?"

"What?"

"You talk more than any woman I've ever known."

"So I've been told. You think that's news?"

"I'm wondering if all this talk was conceivably a buildup, by any slim chance, to a proposal of marriage?"

Her jaw dropped in feigned shock. "Heavens, no. You think just because I'm crazy in love with you that I'd behave like a brazen, shameless hussy? I haven't got a forward bone in my whole body, Zach. I would never, ever, just come on to a man."

"No?" He plucked her close, and pulled her arms around his neck as if he finally, really believed they belonged there. "You took some incredible risks with me from the start, Ms. Grams. I hate to ask you to take another one, but I'm afraid there isn't a prayer I could live without you."

"Me? Freckle-faced, skinny me?" She said thoughtfully, "I might consider a wild fling with a stranger."

"A long-term wild fling?"

"Well . . . how long-term did you have in mind?"

He didn't immediately answer her. At least verbally. He took a kiss that made her think of violets and hyacinths, and then he gave her a second kiss that made her hear music. A spring-soft tender love song that ached to be played. A song she'd never have known...if she hadn't had the extraordinary good luck to find the one man who knew all the chords of her heart.

"Your glasses, sweetheart, are steaming. How about if I take them off and put them where they'll be safe?" He tucked them into his pocket, and kissed her again. That kiss started an ominous, dangerous drumroll in her pulse.

"We're in the woods," she reminded him.

"I know. If you're going to risk a wild fling with a stranger, you'd better be prepared for the consequences for the next sixty, seventy years."

"Heavens, that long?"

"That long. And I think we need a sister for Mellie, maybe two or three. I also think you need a ring. Something big and gaudy. Nothing tame for you. And not diamonds, but something with color, lots of color. You're way too wild for pastels, honey. I'll have to look. It'll be hard to find a sapphire as sassy and bright as you."

"You're just talking to distract me. You think I didn't notice where your hands are? Connor, are you trying to get me in trouble?"

"I'm going to do my best. To be all the trouble you can handle for the rest of our lives. I love you, Kirstin. And I swear—I swear from my heart—that I'll never give you a reason to regret loving me."

As if, Kirstin mused, she had any doubts. Winning his self-respect back had been a battle for Zach, and she suspected it wasn't over yet. But she had faith in him. He was the best man she knew, had ever known, which she would have to tell him often. Right now, though, she simply wanted to show him. Slowly she unzipped his jacket.

It was a little chilly in the woods.

But not that chilly.

She'd keep him warm. Today, tomorrow, and for the rest of their lives together.

* * * * *

Jock, that rascally pirate, isn't through matchmaking yet. Be sure to look for Seth's story, BOTHERED, *available in May— from Silhouette Desire.*

SILHOUETTE®

Desire

MAN of the MONTH 1994

It's the men you've come to know and love... with a bold, new look that's going to make you take notice!

January: *SECRET AGENT MAN*
by **Diana Palmer**

February: *WILD INNOCENCE*
by **Ann Major**
(next title in her SOMETHING WILD miniseries)

March: *WRANGLER'S LADY*
by **Jackie Merritt**
(first title in her SAXON BROTHERS miniseries)

April: *BEWITCHED*
by **Jennifer Greene**
(first title in her JOCK'S BOYS miniseries)

May: *LUCY AND THE STONE*
by **Dixie Browning**
(next book in her OUTER BANKS miniseries)

June: *HAVEN'S CALL*
by **Robin Elliott**

And that's just the first six months! Later in the year, look for books by Barbara Boswell, Cait London, Joan Hohl, Annette Broadrick and Lass Small....

MAN OF THE MONTH...ONLY FROM SILHOUETTE DESIRE

Three new stories celebrating
motherhood and love

Birds, Bees and Babies '94

NORA ROBERTS
ANN MAJOR
DALLAS SCHULZE

A collection of three stories, all by
award-winning authors, selected
especially to reflect the love all
families share. Silhouette's fifth annual
romantic tribute to mothers is sure
to touch your heart.

Available in May,
BIRDS, BEES AND BABIES 1994 is a
perfect gift for yourself or a loved one
to celebrate the joy of motherhood.

**Available at your favorite
retail outlet.**

Only from

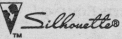

Silhouette®

—where passion lives.

BBB94

IT'S OUR 1000TH SILHOUETTE ROMANCE, AND WE'RE CELEBRATING!

JOIN US FOR A SPECIAL COLLECTION OF LOVE STORIES BY AUTHORS YOU'VE LOVED FOR YEARS, AND NEW FAVORITES YOU'VE JUST DISCOVERED. JOIN THE CELEBRATION...

April
REGAN'S PRIDE by **Diana Palmer**
MARRY ME AGAIN by **Suzanne Carey**

May
THE BEST IS YET TO BE by **Tracy Sinclair**
CAUTION: BABY AHEAD by **Marie Ferrarella**

June
THE BACHELOR PRINCE by **Debbie Macomber**
A ROGUE'S HEART by **Laurie Paige**

July
IMPROMPTU BRIDE by **Annette Broadrick**
THE FORGOTTEN HUSBAND by **Elizabeth August**

SILHOUETTE ROMANCE...VIBRANT, FUN AND EMOTIONALLY RICH! TAKE ANOTHER LOOK AT US! AND AS PART OF THE CELEBRATION, READERS CAN RECEIVE A FREE GIFT!

YOU'LL FALL IN LOVE ALL OVER
AGAIN WITH
SILHOUETTE ROMANCE!

CEL1000

MYSTERY WIFE
Annette Broadrick

She awoke in a French hospital—and found handsome Raoul DuBois, claiming she was his wife, Sherye, mother of their two children. But she didn't recognize him or remember her identity. Whoever she was, Sherye grew more attached to the children every day—and the growing passion between her and Raoul was like nothing they'd ever known before....

She's friend, wife, mother—she's you! And beside each Special Woman stands a wonderfully *special* man. It's a celebration of our heroines—and the men who become part of their lives.

Don't miss **THAT SPECIAL WOMAN!** each month— from some of your special authors! Only from Silhouette Special Edition!

TSW494